# THE NEWS OF THE WORLD

# THE NEWS
# OF THE
# WORLD

STORIES BY

RON CARLSON

*Ron Carlson*

*W·W·NORTON & COMPANY*

NEW YORK        LONDON

Published simultaneously in Canada by Penguin Books Canada Ltd,
2801 John Street, Markham, Ontario L3R 1B4
Printed in the United States of America.


The text of this book is composed in Linotron 202
11 on 14 Garamond No. 3, with display type set in
Bembo, Composition by PennSet, Inc.
Manufacturing by The Haddon Craftsmen, Inc.
Book design by Margaret M. Wagner.


First Edition


Library of Congress Cataloging-in-Publication Data
Carlson, Ron.
The news of the world.
I. Title.
PS3553.A733N4   1987      813'.54      86–5418

ISBN 0-393-02353-2

W. W. Norton & Company, Inc.
500 Fifth Avenue, New York, N.Y. 10110
W. W. Norton & Company Ltd.
37 Great Russell Street, London WC1B 3NU

1 2 3 4 5 6 7 8 9 0

FOR

CAROL HOUCK SMITH

# CONTENTS

## I

THE GOVERNOR'S BALL 15

THE H STREET SLEDDING RECORD 25

SANTA MONICA 36

OLYMPUS HILLS 44

LIFE BEFORE SCIENCE 49

## I I

BIGFOOT STOLE MY WIFE 85

I AM BIGFOOT 91

MADAME ZELENA FINALLY
COMES CLEAN 94

THE TIME I DIED 104

THE USES OF VIDEOTAPE 112

PHENOMENA 116

# Contents

## I I I

*HALF LIFE*     *135*

*MILK*     *150*

*BLOOD*     *165*

*MAX*     *174*

*THE STATUS QUO*     *177*

THE author wishes to thank the National Endowment for the Arts for its generous support.

"Bigfoot Stole My Wife" and parts of section II were performed at the Sundance Playwrights' Institute, thanks to David Kranes and company; at the Ensemble Studio Theatre in New York, thanks to John Rothman and company; at the Philadelphia Festival Theatre, thanks to Carol Rocamora and company; and at the Salt Lake Acting Company, thanks to Ed Gryska and company.

# I

# THE
# GOVERNOR'S
# BALL

*I DIDN'T* know until I had the ten-ton wet carpet on top of the hideous load of junk and I was soaked with the dank rust water that the Governor's Ball was that night. It was late afternoon and I had wrestled the carpet out of our basement, with all my strength and half my anger, to use it as a cover so none of the other wet wreckage that our burst pipes had ruined would blow out of the truck onto Twenty-first South as I drove to the dump. The wind had come up and my shirt front was stiffening as Cody pulled up the driveway in her Saab.

"You're a mess," she said. "Is the plumber through?"

"Done and gone. We can move back in tomorrow afternoon."

"We've got the ball in two hours."

"Okay."

"Could we not be late for once," Cody said. It was the first time I had stood still all day, and I felt how wet my feet were; I wanted to fight, but I couldn't come up with anything great. "I've got your clothes and everything. Come along."

"No problem," I said, grabbing the old rope off the cab floor.

"You're not going to take that to the dump now, are you?"

"Cody," I said, going over to her window, "I just loaded this. If I leave it on the truck tonight, one of the tires will go flat, and you'll have to help me unload this noxious residue tomorrow

15

so I can change it. I've got to go. I'll hurry. You just be ready."

Her window was up by the time I finished and I watched her haul the sharp black car around and wheel into traffic. Since the pipes had frozen, we were staying with Dirk and Evan.

The old Ford was listing hard to the right rear, so I skipped back into the house for a last tour. Except for the sour water everywhere, it looked like I had everything. Then I saw the mattress. I had thrown the rancid king-size mattress behind the door when I had first started and now as I closed the front of the house, there it was. It was so large I had overlooked it. Our original wedding mattress. It took all the rest of my anger and some of tomorrow's strength to hoist it up the stairs and dance it out the back, where I levered it onto the hood of the truck by forcing my face, head, and shoulders into the ocher stain the shape of South America on one side. Then I dragged it back over the load, stepping awkwardly in the freezing carpet.

The rear tire was even lower now, so I hustled, my wet feet sloshing, and tied the whole mess down with the rope, lacing it through the little wire hoops I'd fashioned at each corner of the truck bed.

There was always lots of play in the steering of the Ford, but now, each time it rocked backward, I had no control at all. My fingers were numb and the truck was so back-heavy that I careened down Fifth South like a runaway wheelbarrow. The wind had really come up now, and I could feel it lifting at me as I crossed the intersections. It was cold in the cab, the frigid air crashing through the hole where the radio had been, but I wasn't stopping. I'd worried my way to the dump in this great truck a dozen times.

The Governor's Ball is two hundred dollars per couple, but we went every year as Dirk's guests. The event itself is held at the Hotel Utah, and the asparagus and salmon are never bad, but holding a dress ball in January is a sort of mistake, all that gray cleavage, everyone sick of the weather.

I was thinking about how Dirk always seated himself by Cody, how he made sure she was taken care of, how they danced the first dance, when the light at Third West turned green and I mounted the freeway. As soon as I could, I squeezed way right to get out of everybody's way, and because the wind here was fierce, sheering across at forty miles per hour, at least. The old truck was rocking like a dinghy; I was horsing the steering wheel hard, trying to stay in my lane, when I felt something go. There was a sharp snap and in the rearview mirror I saw the rope whip across the back. The mattress rose like a playing card and jumped up, into the wind. It sailed left off the truck, waving over the rail, and was gone. I checked the rear, slowing. The mattress had flown out and over and off the ramp, five stories to the ground. I couldn't see a thing, except that rope, snapping, and the frozen carpet which wasn't going anywhere.

The traffic around me all slowed, cautioned by this vision. I tried to wave at them as if I knew what was going on and everything was going to be all right. At the Twenty-first South exit, I headed west, letting the rope snap freely, as if whipping the truck for more speed.

The dump, lying in the lea of the Kennecott tailings mound, was strangely warm. Throwing the debris onto the mountain of trash, I could smell certain sweet things rotting, and my feet warmed up a bit. By the time I swept out the truck, it was full dark. I still had half an hour to make the Governor's Ball.

I hit it hard driving away from the dump, just like everybody does, hoping to blow the microscopic cooties from their vehicles, but when I got back to Ninth West, I turned off. I didn't want to go retrieve the mattress; it was nine years old and had been in the basement three. But I had lost it. I had to call Cody.

The first neon I ran across was a place called The Oasis, a bar among all the small industries in that district. Inside, it was smotheringly warm and beery. I hadn't realized how cold my hands were until I tried for the dime in the pay phone. The jukebox was at full volume on Michael Jackson singing "Beat It!" so that when Cody answered, the first thing she said was: "Where are you?"

"I lost the mattress; I'm going to be late."

"What?"

"Go along with Dirk; I'll join you. Don't let anybody eat my salmon."

"Where are you?"

"The mattress blew out of the truck; I've got to go get it. And Cody."

"What?"

"Behave."

It was not until I had hung up that I saw the dancer. They had built a little stage in the corner of the bar and a young girl wearing pasties and a pair of Dale Evans fringed panties was dancing to the jukebox. Her breasts were round and high and didn't bounce very much, though they threw nice shadows when the girl turned under the light. I sat in my own sour steam at the end of the bar and ordered a beer. My fingernails ached as my hands warmed. All the men along the row sat with their backs to the bar to see the girl. I sat forward, feeling the grime melt in my clothes, and watched her in the mirror.

When the song ended, there was some applause, but only from two tables, and the lights on the stage went off. The barmaid was in front of me and I said *no, thanks*, and then she turned a little and said, "What would you like, Terry?"

I realized that the dancer was standing at my elbow. Now she was wearing a lacy fringed pajama top too, and I could see that she was young, there was a serious pimple above one of her eyebrows. I didn't know I was staring at her until she said: "Don't even *try* to buy me a drink." I started to put up my hands, meaning I was no harm, when she added: "I've seen your kind before. Why don't you go out and do some good?"

The barmaid looked at me as if I had started the whole thing, and before I could speak, she moved down to serve the other end.

It was a long walk to the truck, but I made it. January. The whole city had cabin fever. She'd seen my kind before. Not *me*: my *kind*. The old truck was handling better now, and I conducted it back along Ninth West to Ninth South and started hunting. I'd never been under that on-ramp before, except for one night when Cody took me to the Barb Wire, a western bar where we watched all her young lawyer friends dance with the cowboys. In the dark, the warehouses made their own blank city. It was eight o'clock. Cody and Dirk were having cocktails in the Lafayette Suite. She'd be drinking vodka tonics with two limes. Dirk would be drinking scotch without any ice. He would have the Governor's elbow in his left palm right now, steering him around to Cody, "You remember Cody Westerman. Her husband is at the dump."

I crossed under the ramp at Fourth West and weaved under it to the corner of Fifth, where I did a broad, slow U-turn across the railroad tracks to scan the area. Nothing. Two derelicts leaned against the back of a blue post office van, drinking out of a paper sack. I cruised slowly up beside them.

"Hi, you guys," I said. It was the first time all day I felt fine about being so dirty. They looked at me frankly, easily, as if this meeting had been arranged. One, his shirt buttoned up under his skinny chin, seemed to be chewing on something. The other had the full face of an Indian, and I was surprised to see she was a woman. They both wore short blue cloth Air Force jackets with the insignias missing.

"Have you seen a mattress?"

The woman said something and turned to the man.

"What did she say? Have you seen one?"

The man took a short pull on the bottle and continued chewing. "She said, *what kind of mattress is it?*" He passed the bottle to the woman and she smiled at me.

I thought: Okay. What kind of mattress is it. Okay, I can do this. "It was a king-size Sealy Posturepedic."

"King-size?"

"Yes: King-size. Have you seen it?"

He took the bottle back from the woman and nodded at me.

"You have? Where?"

"Would this king-size postropeeda fly out of the sky?" the man said. His eyes were bright; this was the best time he'd had all day.

"It would."

"What's it worth to you?" he said.

"Nothing, folks. I was throwing it away."

"You threw it all right!" the woman said, and they both laughed.

I waited, one arm on the steering wheel, but then I saw the truth: these two were champion waiters; that's what they did for a living.

"Where's the mattress? Come on. Please."

"It's not worth anything."

"Okay, what's it worth?"

"Two bottles of this," the man said, pulling a fifth of Old Grand Dad from the bag.

"That's an expensive mattress."

The man stopped chewing and said, "It's king-size." They both laughed again.

"Okay. It's a deal. Two bottles of bourbon. Where is it?"

For a minute, neither moved, and I thought we were in for another long inning of waiting, but then the woman, still looking at me, slowly raised her hand and pointed over her head. I looked up. There it was, at least the corner of it, hanging over the edge of the one-story brick building: Wolcott Engineering.

Well, that's it, I thought. I tried. Monday morning the engineers would find a large mattress on their roof. It was out of my hands.

The woman stepped up and tapped my elbow. "Back this around in the alley," she said. "Get as close to the building as you can."

"What?"

"No problem," the man said. "We'll get your mattress for you; we got a deal going here, don't we?"

I backed into the alley beside Wolcott Engineering, so close I couldn't open my door and had to slide across to climb out. The woman was helping the man into the bed of the truck, and when I saw it was his intention to climb on the cab of the truck to reach the roof, I stopped him.

"I'll do it," I said.

"Then I'll catch it," he laughed.

The roof was littered with hundreds of green Thunderbird bottles glinting in the icy frost. They clattered under the mattress as I dragged it across to the alley. For a moment, it stood on the edge of the roof and then folded and fell, fainting like a starlet into the cold air.

By the time I climbed down, they had the mattress crammed into the pickup. It was too wide and the depression in the middle formed a nest; the man and the woman were lying in there on their backs. "Two bottles," the man said.

"Don't you want to ride in front?"

"You kidding?"

The Ford's windshield was iced, inside and out, and that complicated my search for a way out of the warehouse district. I crossed sixteen sets of railroad tracks, many twice, finally cutting north through an alley to end up under the Fourth South viaduct. I heard a tap on the rear window. I rolled down my window.

"Could you please drive back across those tracks one more time?"

"What?"

"Please!"

So I made a slow circuit of our route again, rumbling over several series of railroad tracks. I adjusted the mirror and watched my passengers. As the truck would roll over the tracks, the two would bounce softly in the mattress, their arms folded tightly over their chests like corpses, the woman's face absolutely closed up in laughter. They were laughing their heads off. Returning to the viaduct, I stopped. The man tilted his chin up so he looked at me upside down and he mouthed: "Thanks."

I cruised around Pioneer Park, a halo frozen around each street-lamp, and eased into the liquor store parking lot.

"We'll wait here," the man told me.

Inside, I was again reminded of how cold I was, and the clerk shook his head looking at my dirty clothing as I bought the two bottles of Old Grand Dad and a mini-bottle for myself. He clucked as I dropped the change. My jacket pocket had gotten ripped pushing the mattress across the roof; the coins went right through. My hands were cold and I had some difficulty retrieving the money. When I stood, I said simply to the clerk: "These bottles are all for me. I'm going to drink them tonight sleeping under the stars and wake up frozen to Third West. You've seen my kind before, haven't you?"

Outside, I laid the bottles on top of my passengers, one each on their stomachs.

"Many thanks," the man said to me. "It was worth it."

"Where can I let you off?"

"Down at the park, if it's no trouble."

The woman lay smiling, a long-term smile. She turned her shiny eyes on me for a second and nodded. The two of them looked like kids lying there.

I drove them back to the park, driving slowly around the perimeter, waiting for the man to tap when he wanted to get out. After I'd circled the park once, I stopped across from the Fuller Paint warehouse. The man looked up at me upside down again and made a circular motion with his first finger, and then he held it up to signal: just once more.

I opened the mini-bottle and took a hot sip of bourbon. The park, like all the rest of the city was three feet in sooty snow, and some funny configurations stood on the stacks of the old locomotive which was set on the corner. The branches of the huge trees were silver in the black sky, iced by the insistent mist. There were no cars at all, and so I sipped the whiskey and drove around the park four times, slowly. It was quarter to ten; Cody would have given my salmon to Dirk by now, saying something like, "He's been killed on an icy overpass, let's eat his fish and then dance."

I stopped this time opposite the huge locomotive. I stood out beside the bed of the truck. "Is this all right?"

The man sat up. "Sure, son; this is fine." They hadn't opened their new bottles. Then I saw that the woman was turned on her side. Something was going on.

"What's the matter? Is she all right?"

"It's all right," he said, and he helped her sit up. Her face glowed under all the tears; her chin vibrated with the sobbing, and the way her eyes closed now wanted to break my heart.

"What is it? What can I do?"

They climbed over the tailgate of the truck. The woman said something. The man said to me: "We're all right." He smiled.

"What did she say?" I asked him.

"She said thanks; she said, *It's so beautiful. It's so chilly and so beautiful.*"

# THE H STREET
# SLEDDING
# RECORD

*THE* last thing I do every Christmas Eve is go out in the yard and throw the horse manure onto the roof. It is a ritual. After we return from making our attempt at the H Street Sledding Record, and we sit in the kitchen sipping Egg Nog and listening to Elise recount the sled ride, and Elise then finally goes to bed happily, reluctantly, and we finish placing Elise's presents under the tree and we pin her stocking to the mantel—with care—and Drew brings out two other wrapped boxes which anyone could see are for me, and I slap my forehead having forgotten to get her anything at all for Christmas (except the prizes hidden behind the glider on the front porch), I go into the garage and put on the gloves and then into the yard where I throw the horse manure on the roof.

Drew always uses this occasion to call my mother. They ex- change all the Christmas news, but the main purpose of the calls the last few years has been for Drew to stand in the window where she can see me out there lobbing the great turds up into the snow on the roof, and describe what I am doing to my mother. The two women take amusement from this. They say things like: "You married him" and "He's your son." I take their responses to my rituals as a kind of fond, subtle support, which it is. Drew had said when she first discovered me throwing the manure on the roof, the Christmas that Elise was four, "You're the only man I've ever known who did that." See: a compliment.

But, now that Elise is eight, Drew has become cautious: "You're fostering her fantasies." I answer: "Kids grow up too soon these days." And then Drew has this: "What do you want her to do, come home from school in tears when she's fifteen? Some kid in her class will have said—*Oh, sure, Santa's reindeer shit on your roof, eh?*" All I can say to Drew then is: "Some kid in her class! Fine! I don't care what he says. I'm her father!"

I have thrown horse manure on our roof for four years now, and I plan to do it every Christmas Eve until my arm gives out. It satisfies me as a homeowner to do so, for the wonderful amber stain that is developing between the swamp cooler and the chimney and is visible all spring-summer-fall as you drive down the hill by our house, and for the way the two rosebushes by the gutterspout have raged into new and profound growth during the milder months. And as a father, it satisfies me as a ritual that keeps my family together.

Drew has said, "You want to create evidence? Let's put out milk and a cookie and then drink the milk and eat a bite out of the cookie."

I looked at her. "Drew," I had said, "I don't like cookies. I never ate a dessert in my life."

And like I said, Drew has been a good sport, even the year I threw one gob short and ran a hideous smear down the kitchen window screen that hovered over all us until March when I was able to take it down and go to the carwash.

I obtain the manure from my friend Bob, more specifically from his horse, Power, who lives just west of Heber. I drive out there the week before Christmas and retrieve about a bushel. I throw it on the roof a lump at a time, wearing a pair of welding gloves my father gave me.

*I PUT* the brake on the sled in 1975 when Drew was pregnant with Elise so we could still make our annual attempt on the H Street Record on Christmas Eve. It was the handle of a broken Louisville Slugger baseball bat, and still had the precise "34" stamped into the bottom. I sawed it off square and drilled and bolted it to the rear of the sled, so that when I pulled back on it, the stump would drag us to a stop. As it turned out, it was one of the two years when there was no snow, so we walked up to Eleventh Avenue and H Street (as we promised: rain or shine), sat on the Flexible Flyer in the middle of the dry street on a starry Christmas Eve, and I held her in my lap. We sat on the sled like two basketball players contesting possession of her belly. We talked a little about what it would be like when she took her leave from the firm and I had her home all day with the baby, and we talked remotely about whether we wanted any more babies, and we talked about the Record, which was set on December 24, 1969, the first Christmas of our marriage, when we lived in the neighborhood, on Fifth Avenue in an old barn of a house the total rent on which was seventy-two fifty, honest, and Drew had given me the sled that very night and we had walked out about midnight and been surprised by the blizzard. No wonder we took the sled and walked around the corner up H Street, up, up, up to Eleventh Avenue, and without speaking or knowing what we were doing, opening the door on the second ritual of our marriage, the annual sled ride (the first ritual was the word "condition" and the activities it engendered in our droopy old bed).

At the top we scanned the city blurred in snow, sat on my brand new Christmas sled, and set off. The sled rode high and effortlessly through the deep snow, and suddenly, as our hearts

27

started and our eyes began to burn against the snowy air, we were going faster than we'd planned. We crossed Tenth Avenue, nearly taking flight in the dip, and then descended in a dark rush: Ninth, Eighth, Seventh, soaring across each avenue, my arms wrapped around Drew like a straitjacket to drag her off with me if a car should cross in front of us on Sixth, Fifth Avenue, Fourth (this all took seconds, do you see?) until a car did turn onto H Street, headed our way, and we veered the new sled sharply, up over the curb, dousing our speed in the snowy yard one house from the corner of Third Avenue. Drew took a real faceful of snow, which she squirmed around and pressed into my neck, saying the words: "Now, that's a record!"

And it was the Record: Eleventh to Third, and it stood partly because there had been two Christmas Eves with no snow, partly because of assorted spills brought on by too much speed, too much laughter, sometimes too much caution, and by a light blue Mercedes that crossed Sixth Avenue just in front of us in 1973. And though some years were flops, there was nothing about Christmas that Elise looked forward to as much as our one annual attempt at the H Street Sledding Record.


*I THINK* Drew wants another baby. I'm not sure, but I think she wants another child. The signs are so subtle they barely seem to add up, but she says things like, "Remember before Elise went to school?" and "There sure are a lot of women in their mid-thirties having babies." I should ask her. But for some reason, I don't. We talk about everything, *everything*. But I've avoided this topic. I've avoided talking to Drew about this topic because I want another child too badly to have her not want one. I want a little boy to come into the yard on Christmas morning and say: "See, there on the roof! The reindeers were there!" I want another

28

kid to throw horse manure for. I'll wait. It will come up one of these days; I'll find a way to bring it up. Christmas is coming.

Every year on the day after Halloween, I tip the sled out of the rafters in the garage and Elise and I sponge it off, clean the beautiful dark blond wood with furniture polish, enamel the nicked spots on the runner supports with black engine paint, and rub the runners themselves with waxed paper. It is a ritual done on the same plaid blanket in the garage and it takes all afternoon. When we are finished, we lean the sled against the wall, and Elise marches into the house. "Okay now," she says to her mother: "Let it snow."

ON the first Friday night in December, every year, Elise and Drew and I go buy our tree. This too is ritual. Like those families that bundle up and head for the wilderness so they can trudge through the deep, pristine snow, chop down their own little tree, and drag it, step by step, all the way home, we venture forth in the same spirit. Only we take the old pickup down to South State and find some joker who has thrown up two strings of colored lights around the corner of the parking lot of a burned-out Safeway and is proffering trees to the general public.

There is something magical and sad about this little forest just sprung up across from City Tacos, and Drew and Elise and I wander the wooded paths, waiting for some lopsided pinon to leap into our hearts.

The winter Drew and I became serious, when I was a senior and she was already in her first year at law school, I sold Christmas trees during vacation. I answered a card on a dorm bulletin board and went to work for a guy named Geer, who had cut two thousand squat pinons from the hills east of Cedar City and was selling them from a dirt lot on Redwood Road. Drew's mother invited me to stay with them for the holidays, and it gave me the chance to help Drew make up her mind about me. I would sell trees until midnight with Geer, and then drive back to Drew's and watch every old movie in the world and wrestle with Drew until our faces were mashed blue. I wanted to complicate things wonderfully by having her sleep with me. She wanted to keep the couch cushions between us and think it over. It was a crazy Christmas; we'd steam up the windows in the entire living room, but she never gave in. We did develop the joke about "condition," which we still use as a code word for desire. And later, I won't say if it was spring or fall, when Drew said to me, "I'd like to see you about this condition," I knew everything was going to be all right, and that we'd spend every Christmas together for the rest of our lives.

One night during that period, I delivered a tree to University Village, the married students' housing off Sunnyside. The woman was waiting for me with the door open as I dragged the pine up the steps to the second floor. She was a girl, really, about twenty, and her son, about three, watched the arrival from behind her. When I had the tree squeezed into the apartment, she asked if I could just hold it for a minute while she found her tree stand. If you ever need to stall for a couple of hours, just say you're looking for your tree stand; I mean the girl was gone for about twenty minutes. I stood and exchanged stares with the kid, who was scared; he didn't understand why some strange man had brought a tree into his home. "Christmas," I told him. "Christmas. Can you say 'Merry Christmas'?" I was an idiot.

When the girl returned with her tree stand, she didn't seem in any hurry to set it up. She came over to me and showed me the tree stand, holding it up for an explanation as to how it worked. Close up the girl's large eyes had an odd look in them, and then I understood it when she leaned through the boughs and kissed me. It was a great move; I had to hand it to her. There I was holding the tree; I couldn't make a move either way. It has never been among my policies to kiss strangers, but I held the kiss and the tree. Something about her eyes. She stepped back with the sweetest look of embarrassment and hope on her pretty face that I'd ever seen. "Just loosen the turn-screws in the side of that stand," I said, finally. "And we can put this tree up."

By the time I had the tree secured, she had returned again with a box of ornaments, lights, junk like that, and I headed for the door. "Thanks," I said. "Merry Christmas."

Her son had caught on by now and was fully involved in unloading the ornaments. The girl looked up at me, and this time I saw it all: her husband coming home in his cap and gown last June, saying, "Thanks for law school, honey, but I met Doris at the Juris-Prudence Ball and I gotta be me. Keep the kid."

The girl said to me, "You could stay and help."

It seemed like two statements to me, and so I answered them separately: "Thank you. But I can't stay; that's the best help. Have a good Christmas."

And I left them there together, decorating that tree; a ritual against the cold.

*"HOW* do you like it?" Elise says to me. She has selected a short broad bush which seems to have grown in two directions at once and then given up. She sees the look on my face and says, "If you can't say anything nice, don't say anything at all. Besides, I've already decided: this is the tree for us."

"It's a beautiful tree," Drew says.

"Quasimodo," I whisper to Drew. "This tree's name is Quasimodo."

"No whispering," Elise says from behind us. "What's he saying now, Mom?"

"He said he likes the tree, too."

Elise is not convinced and after a pause she says, "Dad. It's Christmas. Behave yourself."

When we go to pay for the tree, the master of ceremonies is busy negotiating a deal with two kids, a punk couple. The tree man stands with his hands in his change apron and says, "I gotta get thirty-five bucks for that tree." The boy, a skinny kid in a leather jacket, shrugs and says he's only got twenty-eight bucks. His girlfriend, a large person with a bowl haircut and a monstrous black overcoat festooned with buttons, is wailing, "Please! Oh no! Jimmy! Jimmy! I love that tree! I want that tree!" The tree itself stands aside, a noble pine of about twelve feet. Unless these kids live in a gymnasium, they're buying a tree bigger than their needs.

Jimmy retreats to his car, an old Plymouth big as a boat. "Police Rule" is spraypainted across both doors in balloon letters. He returns instantly and opens a hand full of coins. "I'll give you thirty-one bucks, fifty-five cents, and my watch." To our surprise, the wily tree man takes the watch to examine it. When I see that, I give Elise four dollars and tell her to give it to Kid Jimmy and say, "Merry Christmas." His girlfriend is still wailing but now a minor refrain of "Oh Jimmy, that tree! Oh Jimmy, etc." I haven't seen a public display of emotion and longing of this magnitude in Salt Lake City, ever. I watch Elise give the boy the money, but instead of saying, "Merry Christmas," I hear her say instead: "Here, Jimmy. Santa says keep your watch."

Jimmy pays for the tree, and his girl—and this is the truth—jumps on him, wrestles him to the ground in gratitude and smothers him for nearly a minute. There have never been people happier about a Christmas tree. We pay quickly and head out before Jimmy or his girlfriend can think to begin thanking us.

On the way home in the truck, I say to Elise, "Santa says keep your watch, eh?"

"Yes, he does," she smiles.

"How old are you, anyway?"

"Eight."

It's an old joke, and Drew finishes it for me: "When he was your age, he was seven."

We will go home and while the two women begin decorating the tree with the artifacts of our many Christmases together, I will thread popcorn onto a long string. It is a ritual I prefer for its uniqueness; the fact that once a year I get to sit and watch the two girls I am related to move about a tree inside our home, while I sit nearby and sew food.

ON THE morning of the twenty-fourth of December, Elise comes into our bedroom, already dressed for sledding. "Good news," she says. "We've got a shot at the record."

Drew rises from the pillow and peeks out the blind. "It's snowing," she says.

Christmas Eve, we drive back along the snowy Avenues, and park on Fifth, as always. "I know," Elise says, hopping out of the car. "You two used to live right over there before you had me and it was a swell place and only cost seventy-two fifty a month, honest."

Drew looks at me and smiles.

"How old are you?" I ask Elise, but she is busy towing the sled away, around the corner, up toward Eleventh Avenue. It is still snowing, petal flakes, teeming by the streetlamps, trying to carry the world away. I take Drew's hand and we walk up the middle of H Street behind our daughter. There is no traffic, but the few cars have packed the tender snow perfectly. It *could* be a record. On Ninth Avenue, Drew stops me in the intersection, the world still as snow, and kisses me. "I love you," she says.

"What a planet," I whisper. "To allow such a thing."

By the time we climb to Eleventh Avenue, Elise is seated on the sled, ready to go. "What are you guys waiting for, Christmas?" she says and then laughs at her own joke. Then she becomes all business: "Listen, Dad, I figure if you stay just a little to the left of the tire tracks we could go all the way. And no wobbling!" She's referring to last year's record attempt, which was extinguished in the Eighth Avenue block when we laughed ourselves into a fatal wobble and ended in a slush heap.

We arrange ourselves on the sled, as we have each Christmas Eve for eight years. As I reach my long legs around these two women, I sense their excitement. "It's going to be a record!" Elise whispers into the whispering snow.

"Do you think so?" Drew asks. She also feels this could be the night.

"Oh yeah!" Elise says. "The conditions are perfect!"

"What do you think?" Drew turns to me.

"Well, the conditions are perfect."

When I say *conditions*, Drew leans back and kisses me. So I press: "There's still room on the sled," I say, pointing to the "F" in Flexible Flyer that is visible between Elise's legs. "There's still room for another person."

"Who?" Elise asks.

"Your little brother," Drew says, squeezing my knees.

And that's about all that was said, sitting up there on Eleventh Avenue on Christmas Eve on a sled which is as old as my marriage with a brake that is as old as my daughter. Later tonight I will stand in my yard and throw this year's reindeer droppings on my very own home. I love Christmas.

Now the snow spirals around us softly. I put my arms around my family and lift my feet onto the steering bar. We begin to slip down H Street. We are trying for the record. The conditions, as you know by now, are perfect.

# SANTA MONICA

*I'M IN THE* King's Head at the end of Santa Monica Boulevard drinking my fourth pint of bitter wondering if maybe I should eat something and just go home. I'm sitting under the window watching one guy play darts against himself, and he's not very good. Judith called and said to meet, so I'll stay. The bitter is good; I haven't been here for a couple of months, so I might as well wait it out. If she doesn't show, maybe she's not in trouble after all.

I'm trying to make a catalogue in my head of all the pubs in Hampstead. It's been two years, but I remember the Three Horseshoes at the High Street, where we'd go and watch the teenagers pick each other up. Monday nights they had poetry readings upstairs. I remember one guy read poems with a dummy; he was a ventriloquist. And there was Sir Something who was ninety-six years old. He read from a book he had published at twenty and talked ironically between the poems about what a stupid young man he had been. It was hilarious, but at the end, he said something like he was glad they had asked him to read, but it was the saddest thing he could remember doing. He had to be helped to a chair. Late that spring they invited Judith to read, but we were packing by then for the return.

Across the street, there was the Bird in Hand, which was full of worn-out working men, and down a block was the King of Bohemia, which was warm and cozy, always half full of older married couples. The women had learned to drink. We had lunch in there on Tuesday's, back in the nook by the aquarium. Across the zebra from the Bohemia was King Henry the Fourth, which was gay and way too small, but they had a little garden. All the men in velvet drinking John Courage, everybody's hands above the table, moving. And then down the street, below the fish-market and the newsstand and the doner-kabob shop, was the simplest pub of all, the Rosslyn Arms, which was where we drank, where we met all the American teachers, and where Gordon would get drunk and finger each new necklace Judith wore—the smashed penny, the Parcheesi tokens—pulling her as close as people get while talking to each other. He was as big as a bear and would always get drunk and offer to "bite her bottom," but he was harmless. He wasn't a writer. It was in the Rosslyn Arms where I learned to play real darts, in fact, where behind the bar, in one of the three cigar boxes, my best darts sit right now.

I order another bitter from the girl, and I notice she's a pretty girl about twenty-six, and I tell myself again: I've got to begin noticing women, but by the time she returns with the pint, I've begun my catalogue again, going way to the top of the High Street, at the corner of the heath, and I'm starting with Jack Straw's Castle. I'm trying to decide whether or not to include The Spaniards, where Judith and I walked only one day, but we were too late for lunch and the staff was all cranky. I feel a hand on my shoulder. Judith lifts my glass and drains the whole pint until I can see her eyes closed through the bottom of the glass.

"Hello, Douglas," she says. "Let's eat later." She leads me outside.

If we were strangers, or acquaintances, or anything less than what we are, whatever that is, I would now ask *What's up?*, but we don't talk that way. There is going to be some theater first, I see, as Judith walks two steps ahead of me across the boulevard, through the park, and down the winding steps to the beach. She's wearing a blue oxford shirt under the brown baggy cardigan I bought her in Hampstead. She always wears clothes from the old days when she meets me.

There aren't many people out, since it's a gray day in February, but there is a brighter band of light on the horizon and a warm breeze comes off the sea. I walk behind Judith and kind of enjoy it; the air feels good and I'm full of beer. The light over the ocean makes it seem as if there is a lot of the day left. It's sunny for brunch in Hawaii. I swing my legs, stepping in every other of her footprints. It feels wonderful to move this way; she can take her time. I don't really want to hear about Reichert or the studio.

Judith walks in a forced jaunt, bunched a little against the weather, her fingers in her sweater pockets.

"You kind of walk like David Niven," I say to her back. I'm suddenly thinking this doesn't have to be a terrible interview; the beer has made me careless. She walks on. I let her go a little farther ahead, and then I follow doing crazy steps: five-foot leaps and then micro-steps, inches apart. Backward steps, duck steps, and then a few real long side steps. She'll see this stuff on the way back.

We approach a couple who have committed themselves to a full-scale beach picnic. They are both sitting on a real checked tablecloth and we hear the man say "Viola!" to the young woman as he pulls a bottle of red wine from a large basket. He is wearing a dark sweater which I see has a large crimson "H" on the front. I've seen him in the story department at Paramount.

Judith stops. "Where are we going?"

As she faces me, I see the new necklace, a silver doodah of

38

some kind. When she first came out, she wore a half pence and a New York subway token. When she finally moved in with Reichert, she made a string with six of my cigarette filters, painted turquoise, to make it look like it was my fault. She wants to show me this new one and holds it out. Taking it in my hand, I am as close to her as I've been in ten months.

"Pretty, right?" I see it is a smashed .38 cartridge. "I found it last week at the bottom of the swimming pool."

We start back, but I steer her higher along the beach. I don't want to see those tracks in the sand after all. "You want to go up to the pier?" I say. "You always like the pier."

"The guy back there, the Harvard guy," Judith says, now walking beside me, "he's at Paramount in the story department."

On the pier I finally ask her why she has the day off. She says that a rat has died in the office and they can't find it even though there are two carpenters taking all the video cabinets apart, and the smell is so bad that Reichert sent everybody home. "He's taking meetings at the house, telling everybody that they're so special he's meeting them in private. Today, it's Jamie Curtis. The smell is bad, but you get used to it. I just couldn't take those two stoned carpenters taking the doors off everything and chuckling their heads off."

We buy ten tokens and go into the arcade. She leads me down all three aisles of video games and then back to the booth where she says to the kid: "Don't you have any of the old games? Where's Space Invaders?"

All the games we've seen have "Mega" in the titles. The kid points out a Donkey Kong game in the corner which has seen a lot of use. Judith makes me go first and then she asks questions: "What do you think the point of this game is?" "Do you think the girl is even worth saving?" I'm trying to concentrate, but the little guy acts drunk. He can't decide which ladder to take, and Judith is beside me doing her show: "Do you think the guy really wants the girl?" I never get him above the second tier. The flaming barrel drops right on our heads.

Then, while she plays, she makes statements. She moves him expertly up the levels and says, "The guy could care less about the girl. He wants to get near the ape. He's just curious." She jumps two barrels at once and says, "See this, the guy only likes the outing; he loves to jump the barrels." He seems to run faster when she plays. Judith takes him all the way to the top three times, but when he reaches the girl, Judith steps back, hands off the controls, and lets the monkey grab them both and close the game. "It's fate," she says. "I'm not getting in the way."

As she starts another session, I slip away, out onto the pier and around to the restrooms. The bumper cars are empty. The kid in his booth sits hunched on the high chair, reading a hunting magazine. Reichert brought us out here when we had first moved. He had pointed at the kid in there and told me not to worry, there was plenty of work in California. Judith had laughed.

Later, after he'd hired Judith at the studio, she and I sometimes came out alone and stood at the end of the pier. It was like being on a great ferry headed west; she'd said that. She had liked California then. A lot of things were happening for her. We'd stand and let the waves break under us.

On the one trip we made to France from London, we'd gone out on the ferry deck in a gray drizzle, and she had said that the first thing she was going to do in St. Tropez was take her shirt off and sunburn her key onto her left breast. And, after a quick check that we were alone, she had opened her shirt, her nipples tight in the cold channel air, and placed the necklace in the spot. Two days later, she did just that, creating a little white shape that looked like that key for a long time. On the ferry that day, she had looked for a minute like a short blond figurehead; she'd said that too.

When I return, Judith is out on the pier rail. She holds up the last token and tells me that I'm not getting my last turn. I know that it will soon be another necklace. She has one like it with a Chucky Cheese token on it which reads, "In Pizza We Trust."

She puts the token in her pocket and turns to the sea. The day here is shot, the sun gone, the cloud cover a bald dusk, but in the far west that fuzzy line of light persists on the sea's edge.

"They're having brunch on the veranda in Waikiki."

"I'm as far West as I go." Judith says into the wind. "This is it for me."

I don't want to argue with her. It is a relief not wanting to argue. It is not my fault she came to California. I don't want to say that again. I don't want to attack Reichert or defend him or any of the dozen other people we both still see, all of them bright, well-educated, charming people, mostly young, and every one of them integrally involved in film projects that are hideous or silly. I won't argue. It is a relief. All I want is a beer. I want to push off this rail and walk back, swinging my legs, feeling my knees as we climb the steps, and go back across the street and have another beer.

"You think it's possible to write a good movie?" Judith says, turning to me.

"I think it's less possible than a year ago."

"Oh good, I can't wait until tomorrow."

I nearly say *Neither can I*, but that is exactly how we used to talk. I say: "Judith, let me buy you a pint of bitter and a sandwich."

"You think this is a good country? You think this is a livable country?"

I am not going to do this. "Judith, I can't go on without a

pint," I say, stepping away from the rail. It is an old joke from London. I walk back to the first silver owl, as Judith calls the coin-operated binoculars on the pier.

Way out there I can see the guy from Paramount leaning back on one elbow drinking wine in the gray wind. Where do they learn that stuff? I close my eyes. I try to remember the name of the pub in Highgate across from Coleridge's grave. I can't get it. We walked there once on Easter, up through the cemetery where we stood before Marx's tomb, and now I'm trying to remember Marx's tomb: "Workers of the World Unite, ours is not to something something, but to change something." There was a green-headed mallard on every stone crucifer. Judith and I sat on a green bench in the park and argued about something. The ducks were all mating, walking in circles around us, and then we walked up to the pub which had been a real coach stop in the old days, and it's name was. I can't remember.

I can remember Judith, after she started writing for Reichert, coming home late in the car. She wouldn't come in the house. I would go out after a while and find her sitting in the Rabbit, listening to the end of a Jackson Browne tape. I should have known. It was Reichert's tape: "Hold Out." It was the Era of Maximum Smiling; she called it that. She'd look up from the car and smile. "This is the Era of Maximum Smiling," she'd say.

I wanted then to remind her that the Era of Quality Smiling was when we could watch the kites on Parliament Hill on the heath, when we could see all of London grumbling beneath us, when we would smile at the idea of writing in California. But it was too late. When a woman sits in the car listening to tapes, it's too late.

I walk almost to the second silver owl when Judith catches up. We step back onto the continent, cross the beach, and by the time we're at the top of the stairs, she's taken my arm. She doesn't speak except to say, "David Niven's dead," as we cross the street and go into the King's Head.

At the table, it starts. Her face, and I see again that it is a good face, the only face, falls. When she leans forward to take her face in her hands, I can see the silver cartridge again and all the little red marks above her breasts where her jewelry had nicked her over the years. I remember that after she'd shower it looked like a light coral necklace there. "God, Doug," she says. "I don't know whether to go forward or backward anymore." She's about to cry.

I feel the old numbness rise in my neck, the old bad confusion. I'm glad the girl has brought the wonderful brown beer, and I lift my glass in my hand. The beer is cool and sweet.

"Judith," I say.

"Doug, remember that bitch at the Spaniards who wouldn't serve us because we were five minutes late for pub hours?"

"No," I say. There is no sense in starting. I could ask her now the name of that pub at Highgate, the coach stop, Judith would remember. But: no.

The King's Head is empty now: four o'clock. By seven, every English starlet on the coast will be in here. "Judith. Hey. Don't cry." I push her glass across so it just touches her elbow. "Judith. Here. Drink this. How about the turkey sandwich?"

She nods, her head in her hands.

"Don't cry," I say. "It's possible to write a good movie. It's a livable country. Judith, you are the most clever woman I ever met. But, you were right about that little guy. He doesn't want the girl. He wants to run back and forth. He wants to jump the barrels and not get burned."

# OLYMPUS HILLS

*I LEFT* the party early, finding my coat on the bed, surprising Karen and Darrel, who stood when I entered. "It's funny," I said, trying to ease their embarrassment, "but I know every coat in this pile." I lifted Cindy's rabbit fur jacket. "For five points. Careful: she does not wear this thing to work."

"Cindy," Karen said, her voice husky.

I had just left Cindy in the kitchen. She and Tom were sitting on the counter drinking tequila and having a heart to heart. Whenever people drink tequila, they always talk about it, the worm, a war story or two, and then maybe mushroom experience and it's a heart to heart. Cindy was wearing a white silk dress, sprayed with little red dots which turned out to be strawberries. I have been in these kitchens before and when Cindy hoists her bottom onto the kitchen counter and, nursing a tequila and lemon between her knees, starts telling drug experiences, it's just enough. Even Tom sitting up there by her looked a little spent. He's too big a guy to sit on a kitchen counter and look natural anyway.

Karen and Darrel had forgotten to let go of each other's hands and their faces were smashed red from all the kissing. They looked like the two healthiest people at the party. I was surprised, because I'd seen Karen with another guy from the firm, a programmer named Chuck who does our board overlays, at a dozen lunches in the last month. And I admired Darrel's ability to struggle in there with Karen, while we could all hear his wife, Ellen, singing along with Tommy James and the Shondells in the other room. It was a small house for Olympus Hills.

"Victor, Ted, Sharon, Tom, Ellen," I said, laying the coats aside, until I found the tan raincoat. "Lisa," I said, looking at it. The bed was a little archaeology of the party: all those layers of beautiful coats. Victor and his new leather flight jacket. Tom and his bright swollen parka. And Lisa's classy raincoat second from the bottom. She must have arrived early.

"My coat," I looked up and said to Darrel, and when I saw how embarrassed he still was, leaning there against the wall as if I was going to scold them, I added, "I'm leaving early. No problem." I patted my coat. "I'd say you've got an hour before another coat is touched. I'll close the door. Happy Valentines."

I didn't put my coat on in the hall, because I didn't want Ted or Sharon to make a fuss, to cry out, "Hal, you're leaving! Before charades! You can't leave before charades!"

I wanted to leave before charades. I'd played charades with this group before and it was worse than college. Victor, Ted, and about five others played solely to humiliate everyone. They would select unproduced plays from Gilbert and Sullivan, and then explode when people would claim to have not heard of them. "You ignorami!" I'd heard Victor scream. "You aborigines! Swinesnouts! This is incredible."

My wife, Lisa, could be wicked too. She would always write the sexiest titles she could, knowing that some woman on the other team, in the drunken spirit of camaraderie that sometimes waved over the group, would embarrass herself fully doing *How to Make Love to a Man* and be the talk of the office for a week. I remember in detail the vision of Cindy writhing before the group one night, clutching both her breasts with her hands, thrusting her pelvis at her team as if to drive them back on the couch. I don't remember the name of the literary work she was describing.

I wanted to slip through the living room as if I were getting some fresh air and then be gone. Lisa had come from work tonight and she had her own car; I'd see her at home later. There was a time when we had one car, and we used to go places together. It was a used silver Tempest, the car I had in graduate school. The original owner had applied zodiac stickers in circles on all the doors.

Lisa always claims to hate these parties. We'll be dressing at home and she'll wave the hairdrier at me, making predictions. "Karen will wear that blue mini and go after Lou. They'll have a clam dip diluted with sour cream. Generic sour cream. Did I say generic sour cream? Wayne will move in on me when I sit on the couch and tell me about his kids for two hours. He thinks that's the way you flirt. Ted will bring his oldies tape. Ellen will be the first one to sing. Tom will be the first one drunk. You'll get drunk too and come on to Cindy, and we'll have our little quarrel on the way home. Are you ready? Let's go."

And she used to be right. I would get drunk. I'd end up singing with Ellen and, later, making my three point five crass comments to some of the women. Wayne would do his sincerity routine for Lisa on the couch. He was no dummy; she was always the loveliest woman in the whole house. I'd end up in the kitchen, leaning against the counter with Cindy, sometimes leaning against Cindy and then the counter. It was a party, wasn't it?

That was then. Lisa wouldn't be right tonight, about me. February. It had been a long winter already: five, six parties since New Year's. No wonder Karen had been able to spot Cindy's coat. Too much snow, too much fog; by Friday night, no one wanted to go home. Everybody was kind of surprised suddenly to have money, but no one knew what to do about it. Most of us had Ted's oldies tape memorized the way you come to know an album; when a song ends, you know what's coming next. We knew what brand everyone smoked and who would lend you a cigarette gladly. We knew that Ted smoked Kools because he'd learned in college that no one would borrow them. We knew what everyone drank and how much. We knew where people would be sitting by eleven o'clock. I knew it all and I just wanted to go home. I was trying.

I eased by a group standing by the kitchen door, and edged around the two couples dancing to the Supremes. Ellen waved at me from across the buffet table with the breadstick she was using as a microphone. Baby Love. I could see Lisa sitting on the couch. She was smiling at Wayne who sat on the carpet by her knees. I know all her smiles and this was a real one. I had to thread between Victor and his new girlfriend to reach the door and then I was out in the snow.

Pulling on my coat, I walked down the trail in the falling snow, right into the deer. I didn't actually hit him, but by the time we both looked up we were at most three feet apart. It was a young male. He had a fine pair of forked antlers and a broad black nose, wet and shiny in the light from the yard lamp. I immediately backed up four or five steps to give him room, but he stood there, casually, looking at me. There were deer all over the city because of the snowfall, but I had never, ever, seen one this close.

I backed to the door, slowly, thinking to show someone. I forgot myself. I wanted Lisa to come out and see this guy. I wanted Lisa to come out and see this deer and come home with me. She could say, "We'll pick up my car tomorrow or the day after that," and steam up the dark with her laugh. I hadn't realized how lonely I was until I saw his face, his moist eyes, the bone grain of his antlers.

47

I pushed the door inward and said, "Hey, come see this deer."
Cindy's face appeared in the opening. Behind her the party seemed
to rage; Ellen was singing "Satisfaction," and the din of conversation was loud and raw and alien.

"What?"

"Look at this deer."

"What are you talking about?"

I let the door close and stepped back out. She followed me.
"What are you talking about?"

"This deer." I turned and he was gone. I stepped to the corner
of the house and was able to glimpse his gray back pass under a
yard lamp two houses up.

"Right," Cindy said, taking my arm. "The deer." She lobbed
her drink, glass and all, into the snowbank, and turned fully to
me. Her mouth was warm with tequila, and I could feel the flesh
of her back perfectly through the cold silk of her dress. She rose
against me, ignoring the cold, or frantic against it, I couldn't
tell which. It was funny there outside the party. When she went
for me, I did nothing to stop her. I had made it outside, leaving
early, but that was all I could do.

# LIFE BEFORE
# SCIENCE

*"Yeah, I know about babies."*
— J O H N   W A Y N E
in *THE SANDS OF IWO JIMA*

*IN FEBRUARY*, I drove Story to New Haven for the post-coital. It was Sunday, and if you want a definition of sterility, try downtown New Haven on the second Sunday in February. The clouds were frozen like old newspapers into the sky, and the small parking lot of the clinic was blasted with frozen litter too. I remember there were a pair of old work gloves in the ice. Looked like somebody trying to get out.

Dr. Binderwitz was meeting us on Sunday because Story had been keeping the basal charts for three months and we had to do the post-coital before Binderwitz, the most prominent fertility expert in the known world, flew off to Houston, Rio, Paris, and Frankfurt to deliver papers at conventions. It was a dark day and the doctor had all the lights in the clinic turned on. The doctor himself is one of the least healthy human beings I have ever met. He is a person who has literally spent years indoors, not grooming. When we shook hands, I was surprised at how soft his hand was, and up close, I could see that his hair was sprinkled with dandruff

49

and larger particles I took to be bits of paper and pillow feather. So there we were with this force-ten genius, anxious to hear what he'd say.

The doctor took Story into the examination room, and I sat with a copy of *Sports Afield*, for a moment angry with the cover artist for making his rearing grizzly so predictable. He'd used all his light in the mouth, even spraying some white points of saliva, and that, coupled with the point of view (from below, as a victim) cancelled any real life or sympathy from the work. It was a cheap shot done in half a day by some ad illustrator. There was no setting for the portrait, except a single pine, and that had been drawn melodramatically small. It looked like a folded umbrella.

I was daydreaming. It was still early in the morning. Story had moved to me long before dawn and we'd made lost, unconscious love. It wasn't until after I'd rolled out of bed and stood under the shower that I realized we were participating in an experiment.

Story returned, calling me back to the doctor's office, and then Dr. Binderwitz himself shuffled in, carrying the small prepared slide. He had taken a smear from Story's cervix, and we watched as he positioned the slide under the microscope. Dr. Binderwitz studied the slide for a minute or two and then asked Story if she wanted to have a look. He told her what knob to rotate for focus.

Then it was my turn. By slowly rotating the control, I was suddenly able to see dozens, maybe hundreds of sperm swimming around. I could see the problem right away. "They're not all going the same way," I said. "Which is the right direction?"

It was a little joke, but the doctor said, "They're not supposed to. Do you see the ones with two tails?"

I bent to the eyepiece again and, after a moment I did see a couple of two-tailed sperm whipping around.

"Is that normal?"

"Sure."

"Well," I said, when the doctor was silent, "How does it look?"

"Normal. The sperm are alive. The medium is hospitable." To Story he said, "Call my office Monday and schedule a histogram early next month. I'll be back then."

## T W O

SINCE it was Sunday, there were Township Cocktails that night, this time at Annette and Hugo Ballowell's place on the big lake, Mugacook, right across from the college. It had been a long day, but Story was mayor of the town and there would be some skating on the lake later, so we went down.

It was at Township Cocktails at the Ballowells that February night that I first had a glimpse of what the next four months would hold for us. It was that night that I first saw the solution, the radical answers to this baby thing, though I didn't know it at the time, and it was that night when I came to understand there was a little more to the world than Dr. Binderwitz, even from his intellectual stratosphere, could see.

I don't really know how it happened, the specific point where I left my senses for . . . my senses. I was in a mild funk that had been solidifying over the last year or so as my painting dried up. McOrson was still selling a few every month in New York, but they were old paintings, some of them over two years and they were the skies, the landscapes at which I had become facile, and which I had come to loathe. The reality was simple: I wasn't painting and it hurt. So I wasn't really in a party mood, especially with all the driving, two hours to New Haven, two hours back, and now: cocktails.

Story dressed and drove us down and we ran into Gil Manwaring, the constable, on Foundry Road along the fish pond and he and his two men were parking cars. Story said no thanks and we parked it ourselves and walked four hundred yards in the icy brown dusk, carrying our skates.

The Ballowells' house is the biggest on Mugacook, the kind of place mistaken for an inn by forty cars every summer. Story and I immediately ran into Ruth Wellner, the county attorney, who had been a classmate of Story's in Boston and who was now Story's best friend in Bigville. Ruth and Billy were our age, and were in the first stages of chasing a baby down themselves. Ruth wanted children almost as much as we did, but she couldn't admit it. She played devil's advocate. Ruth used to challenge me: "You want children; *you* have them." She'd go on: "Why do we want kids? What are we going to do with children? Every time we want kids, we ought to get in the car and drive down to K Mart in Torrington. Stay half an hour and we'll get more parenthood than we bargained for."

Billy, whom I liked a lot and who is living proof that insurance agents are human beings too, sat on the arm of the couch wearing an expression the most prominent feature of which was its profound sperm-loss pallor. I winked at Billy and he nodded back stiffly, a gesture he'd seen a battle-weary soldier make in some World War II movie. I admired his courage and Ruth's. The feature of Clomid we all found most unique was the headache each dosage inspired, making intercourse impossible, an irony lost on the chemists.

There is something about women on fertility drugs, something I admire, I suppose, something that gives them an aura: larger than life. It's hard to explain, but it would be easy to paint. I stood to the side a little as Story and Ruth fell to rapt conversation, their voices the rich female timbre that by its very sound says: hey, we're calm here; something mature is transpiring. They could have been talking about the township or about the mysteries of estrogen; it was all music to me. I grabbed Billy's arm. "Let the wives talk, Billy," I said. "I'll buy you a cocktail."

Annette had a buffet that would have run twelve pages in *Ladies' Home Journal*. It started with a salmon the size of a dog and ended forty feet later with champagne and hot buttered rum. Luckily, Hugo was down at that end of the table sipping his scotch, and when I nodded at it he took us in the kitchen and poured us coffee cups full of Chivas, saying, "I never drank a party drink in my life. It's February and this," he held up his glass, "is scotch. Are you two going skating?"

And we did go skating, Hugo, Bill, and I. We had another cup of scotch and then clambored down with Hugo's hockey equipment, sticks and pucks. The moon had come out full and throwing down a couple of sweaters on one side and two hats on the other, we had a rink. For some reason we had constructed it such that the bonfire was at center ice, and the game was full of wonderful breathers while some hero stickhandled the puck back out of the embers. Then, finally, Bill himself skated full bore into the flames. He rolled out unhurt, but he had lost the puck fully in the fire and we stood around consoling him while it melted somewhere in the inferno.

"Showboat," Hugo said, smiling. He looked at me and said, "Remember the night Billy skated into the bonfire?" and he laughed, so sure and so happy to be on the spot as a memory was created, his party a success.

"And he did it showing off!" I said.

53

"And then he wanted more scotch," Billy said, getting up. "He lost the puck and then wanted more scotch. And none of your party drinks!"

Back at the mansion, the party had more than half fallen apart, but Annette and Story and Ruth were in the study grinding something over, so Hugo did pour us some more scotch. We stood around the kitchen like prep school kids when Hugo said, "Let me show you something."

Now, it's here, I guess, where I started to see again. We were all red-faced from the cold and warm from the scotch, and when Hugo ushered me in front of the telescope, it was time to see. He had lined it up so that the full moon filled the lens, and for a moment I was flooded with vertigo, my depth perception thrown away. Then it all twisted into a focus so sharp I winced. The moon, the ocher plains, the pale blue seas, and then like something scratching across my very eyeball, the geese. Canadian geese were flying across the moon. Four clipped the bottom. Two more, sliding. Silence. My heart in my neck. And then two full tiers, a double-winged vee of geese raking the moon, swimming into the heat which rose into my eye and blurred.

I stood away from the telescope.

"Did you see them? They must be three miles high!" Hugo took my arm. It was dark in his study. Billy bent to the eyepiece. I could hear the women murmuring below us in the den. "Do you know how far, how many miles they'll go tonight?"

And it was later, late into that Sunday night—Monday morning—that the seeing began in earnest. Story drove me home, and though it took a few minutes to rid her mind of township business, I achieved it, and we moved into the postures of lovemaking, and I saw her face, her eyes, her navel, and then just before my eyes rolled up into my head, I saw my three fingers coming over Story's shoulder, like three old men witnessing giants at play. Story kissed me and rolled into sleep. My eyes would not quit.

I walked through my house naked for a while, as is the right of any homeowner, ending up on the small brick porch onto the backyard with my father's Navy binoculars in my hand. The air was still and frigid, but I stood with the glasses on the moon. It was wonderfully clear to me there as the bricks froze my feet and my genitals shrank and numbed in the frosty night: sperm were swimming across the moon, and on the round world I had a lot to do.

## T H R E E

FOR three months Story had been keeping the basal charts. When the alarm would sound, I would stumble to the bureau, shake down the thermometer and offer it to Story's sleeping face. She slept on her stomach with no pillow and for eighty days at least, that thermometer was the first thing she saw every day. She'd lie there while I said, "Okay, now, don't move. Two minutes and forty seconds to go. I'm watching you. You're moving. Please. Can you please lie still for two and a half minutes! Okay. I'm telling Doctor Binderwitz that your chart is a fabrication. Two minutes. Fine, fine, squirm around; do your calisthenics; see if I care." It would get down to 10–9–8–7–6–5 and I'd move around and find the glass tube snug in her sleeping mouth. I'd sit on her and announce: "Ninety-eight point nine. We're talking impending ovulation. We're moving into a period of massive fertility!"

She'd groan and say, "Get off me."

"You don't mean that."

Then, every other day, as part of our program, I'd throw my feet up in her side of the bed and she would pull me to her, moving from a warm sleep to the warm, insistent dreamarama lovemaking. She was always a morning person as far as sex was concerned, and it was a smooth, slow swimming which left us both wet eyed, awash, and stunned.

*BIGVILLE* is a small college really, and they are glad to have me because they consider me not just an art teacher, but a *real* painter, that is, one who has two paintings in national collections and one who from time to time has a show on some second floor in New York and a carload of deans gets to go down and drink wine for an afternoon. No one knows I'm not painting, except Story, and as always, she treats me as if I've simply taken some well-earned time off for coffee.

I threw myself into my teaching with an organized enthusiasm that cautioned me. I made progress charts for each of my students, making notes on approaches, even encouraging the oppressive Mary Ann Buxton, who tried too hard to make Bigville into the finishing school she never attended. Her approach to painting was simple: it was something you owned, the way rich people own France during those cocktail parties on campus in the fall. They bought the experience, as if it were a stereo system or a fine meal. I noted happily that Mary Ann was doing less copying and more "emulation" of her neighboring easels. What I am saying is that I did what I could to make the spring into a positive sojourn for myself, despite the fact that my eyes were on fire, seeing things, and I knew that meant something would come of it. But as of March, I was not painting.

The ice on Mugacook began to rot, and sometime mid-month Fudgie Miller fell entirely through a section by the town wharf, ending the skating season for good. Fudgie, twelve, was one of the eight Miller kids who lived right across the road from us, and when Constable Manwaring drove Fudgie home wrapped in a blanket and shivering, he was received with the general joy and jumping up and down usually reserved for only children. I witnessed the crowd scene from my front porch, and I thought: that's it. That's what we're after right there. All right. Now all I need is eight kids.

Because of the headaches, we abandoned Clomid, that wonderdrug, and we drove back down to New Haven on a windy, tree-tearing day in late March for the histogram. The air was thick with rushing grit as we crossed the clinic parking lot, and a copy of the *Yale News* blew against my leg, the headline, as always: STRIKE!

Again I scanned the covers of *Sports Afield* in the waiting room, while the dye was injected through Story's uterus and up into her fallopian tubes. Each of the magazines I had selected bore covers of large fish (two trout and one bass) standing on their tails in a raw white splash. The bass was trying to spit out a salamander plug and each of the trout had an oversized Royal Coachman hooked in the corner of his mouth. I was surprised by how vital, kinetic, and primary each was, and they evoked in me sentiments usually tapped only by top forty hits from the fifties. I love art. Each painter had captured the look of death on a game fish face, and yet he left the viewer one small bright hope: the fish might get away.

Then the nurse came and took me to Story, dressed by now, and we watched the television monitor and the X-ray scan of Story's secret chambers. It was, by far, the best program I've ever seen on television. Story's tubes were clear and symmetrical, the shadow swelling at the end of each tube a bit like an antler in what the technician called the *fibrililium*, a word I had him spell.

We drove halfway home, up Route 8, before we understood

that we felt bad. It was one of those half raw March days, the wind warm where it came around the sunny corner of a building and cold everywhere else. It blew Story's hair in her face as we came out of DeRusso's after a late lunch of hot Italian sausage for which they are famous. When she pulled her hair back, I could see that she was crying. In the car she said: "There's nothing wrong with us." She was right. She'd done the progesterone count twice and hers was *slightly* low, but nothing was wrong. My sperm count was *slightly* low, but still there were millions. Story's uterus was *slightly* tipped, but it shouldn't, in the doctor's words, present a problem. *Science*, I thought. Now there's a word. *Science*. We stopped at Outskirts, the little package store on the edge of Winstead for a roadkit of cold Piels light.

"Here," I said, handing Story a beer. "No ice, no twist of lemon, but a woman who is thirsty has nothing for tears." It was an old joke of ours and she smiled. But the rest of the way home, we felt bad. There was nothing wrong with us and we felt bad.

## F O U R

*I HAD* class the day Story went down to New Haven for her cervical biopsy. I told her I'd cancel, but she insisted on driving down alone. It was the final day of watercolors, before we went on to Life Class with pencils and acrylics, and I had to put up with Mary Ann Buxton gushing about how much she had loved the medium and ya-da, ya-da about her plans to explore it further on her own this summer at her parents' place in Maine, the light there was so delicate and terrific, and la-di-da. I had to walk three easels away to get her to let up. I had to admit, however, she had done a fair job on the four birches that grew beside the Dean's garden. I see the four birches that grow beside the Dean's garden almost twenty times in a year in every possible medium, especially watercolor, and they have almost cancelled my ability to enjoy trees at all. Simply: I hate them. If I stay at Bigville, there will certainly come an evil night when I make their final rendering with a chainsaw.

By the end of class, I'd grown glum, worrying about Story, and I sulked through the easels like a panhandler. It makes you feel funny sometimes as a teaching artist to see your students march through their paces, their work not great, not bad, but *work* anyway: finished paintings. I went back to the four birches. I helped Mary Ann Buxton add a little more light to the upside of a dozen leaves, but I felt like a phony anyway. I needed to paint.

I was home by two and my funk had me nailed to a chair in the dark living room, unable to blink. Luckily, Billy Wellner came by. He'd been to lunch with Ruth and had three beers and didn't want to write any more policies that afternoon. We took off our shirts and played the World Series of one on one in my driveway: best of seven. For an insurance agent, Billy has a good jumpshot, but he rarely drives for the basket and he's all right hand. I beat him four straight and walked him to his car.

Across the street, Mudd Miller himself came onto his porch and began bellowing the names of his children. There were long pauses followed frequently by a name he'd already called.

Billy threatened a rematch and said, "Let us know how Story is."

Half an hour later, I heard the car in the driveway, but Story didn't come in. I found her sitting in the driver's seat, washed out and pale. She made a grim little smile. "I should have had you come," she said. "It's the only thing so far that's hurt. I could hardly use the clutch on the way home."

I took her in and put her to bed. "You're all slimy," she said.

"Sweaty. I'm all sweaty. Since I can't paint, I'm putting my energies into basketball. Does it hurt now?"

"Just a small fire. I think they used a fingernail clippers."

I called the Wellners. Ruth answered and I told her about Story and asked her to handle the Township tomorrow. Before hanging up I gave her the accurate score of this afternoon's basketball massacre. "Why is the world all women and *boys?*" she said. "You take good care of Story; I'll handle the office."

Later still, Dr. Binderwitz's secretary-assistant Michelle called and said that the biopsy showed nothing, that Story was all right. It was a great spring twilight, I could hear the one nightingale calling from Mugacook, and the voices of children playing tag on the edge of the campus, but when I looked in on my sleeping wife, a powerlessness so profound swept over me that I felt my back knotting up. I wanted to shake her shoulder and whisper: "I'll solve this problem," the way a husband should about an incorrect billing or a loose window or a gummy carburetor. I leaned against the doorway that spring night, and I knew the truth: *I couldn't do anything about this.* I couldn't paint or make us have a baby. I could throw a jump shot in from the corner, but as Ruth said, that is a matter for boys.

Story slept. The examination had told us again: she was all right. I folded my arms and felt them tingle with a tension that was new to me; I know now it was the blood sense that I was getting closer.

## F I V E

*BIGVILLE* has, just as it has a Volunteer Fire Department, a volunteer baseball team, which is one of the oldest institutions in the township. And one of the customs that has grown up with our team is that the mayor throws out the ball for the opening game, which is always played at home against New Hartford.

At one in the afternoon on the day after her laparoscopy, Story stood up on the first row of the silly little bleachers in Bigville Park and threw a brand new Bradley baseball to Mudd Miller, who plays catcher for the ball team. He was standing inside the baseline, so it was a fine toss by a woman who had just twenty-four hours prior had a laparoscopy. In fact, when Mudd came over ceremoniously to hand Story back the baseball, he commented that she had more on the ball than any mayor in his fifteen years catching.

Ruth sat with us, being solicitous of her friend Story; she let me know just with her posture that Story's discomfort was somehow all my fault and that she, Ruth, was fundamentally alarmed that a person of my caliber would even try to impose his twisted gene pool onto another generation. Besides her motto about all the kids at K Mart, she always said to Story, while I was in the room; "Why would you want a child, when you're married to one?" However, there was a look of genuine concern on the county attorney's face today, so I could take her cheap heat and watch the ballgame.

During a laparoscopy, a probe is inserted near the navel and searches the fallopian tubes for obstructive material, primarily known as endometriosis. Dr. Binderwitz had been able to tell us that the search had shown nothing, no obstruction. Story's tubes were clear. The operation left a tiny wrinkled scar under her navel, as if to underline it, an emphatic italic of her beauty.

The field was full of townspeople, tradesmen, and friends. Billy was straightaway in right field. Mr. Cummings from the food center was at second base, and one of the deans from the college was on the mound.

The baseball game was tight until the top of the ninth when a bearded man who works in the Sinclair in New Hartford hit a change-up over the old railroad trestle scoring three runs. Bigville couldn't match that, and after the game, Story and I walked the mile home.

"What are we going to do?" Story asked.

"Find a better pitcher; move the dean to the outfield."

She grabbed me around the neck in a mock wrestling hold. I tried to duck out, restrain her arms.

"Careful, one of us just had an operation." I took her hand and we walked on. "Is that the last test?"

"Yes," she said. "And there's nothing wrong with us." The two of us kicked stones along the old road, like two teenagers walking home from school. It was full May, two weeks past even the last cold rain, and the blossoming trees drooped into our path. I could see four men dragging the diving raft toward the lake down at the Grove. Tomorrow, Sunday, some lucky ten-year-old would climb the twenty red rungs on that wooden platform and commit the first cannonball into Mugacook for the summer season.

"What do we do?" Story whispered.

"Keep our chins up." I said. "Interact sexually . . . and . . ."

"What?"

"I don't know. Something else. It'll come to me. Something else."

Story took my arm. "I love you," she said. "I'm sorry we can't have children, but I still and will always love you."


*WHEN* you hold a woman you know quite well, press her softly into, say, a mattress, one hand under her neck, the other on the swelling of her hip, her skin so smooth as to seem forbidding and inviting at the same time, if she moves once, say to reach under your arm and to pull you forward, your mind will go right on by progesterone counts and histograms into a warm lyric zone where it will disappear in a dandy stinging swelter.

In such a swelter, my limbs lost in Story's, one night in May, at a moment when my eyes were about to roll away, I again saw my three fingers come creeping over Story's shoulder; and in the blurred proximity of the warm moment, they looked like the same three blank-faced old men arriving to witness our coupling. At the time I thought it was an odd vision for such a crucial time, but it was the beginning of an odd era, a time when cause–effect would take on new meaning, when order, sequence, science would whirl away.

That night when we rolled apart, I first dreamed of moons and geese and drowning, and then sometime late in the night I saw a perfect and vivid vision:

A man wearing a turquoise steerhead with jeweled horns does a low, steady hop around a campfire, swinging a stone phallus on a gold chain and singing with the insistent drums: HAH-MAH, LOH-LAH, HAH-MAH, LOH-LAH! He stops. He twists a glass vial of some thin red nectar onto the flames. They reach up in a hissing flash and light the area. In the new flare, the man thrusts his painted hand into the abdomen of a splayed chicken, tosses the entrails out in a splash, and begins—as the fire crawls back down to the logs—to read the throw, fingering the shiny organs apart as his shiny eyes begin to fill with the future.

I won't say much about the next few days, except that I did not start painting. I spent all my free time between morning and afternoon classes in the library and the library annex. With the good weather, the buildings were empty, all the undergraduates gone outside to court, and my research was simple. After I exhausted the campus libraries, I went down to Bigville Memorial, built of hewn granite and given to the town by Hugo Ballowell's great grandfather. I spent more than one day there, in fact, I used up the rest of May, not even looking up as the light changed at midday or in the evening, and I ended up in a corner of the basement. I found everything. The two volumes I selected had to be catalogued before I could take them home. *The Dark Arts* and *Life Before Science*. Together they weighed twelve pounds. Mrs. Torrey looked at me as if I was unhinged while I waited for her to write the library cards, but the heft of those books as I hauled them down to my studio seemed the first real thing in my quest. At last, I thought, I am finally doing something.

## S I X

*I ROWED* the boat into dark Mugacook. Okay. Okay. Okay. Now. I've done all my homework. The first sperm to reach the ovum is the only one to enter. Of the millions of sperm sent out, only hundreds reach the ovum, and only the first to touch it enters. Upon entering, he swells and bursts, spilling the twenty-three chromosomes he's been carrying. That part is beyond me.

I rowed the old red rowboat and said aloud, "Okay, okay, okay."

When I perceived I was in line with the lighted church spire in town and the dozen lights of the Ballowell main house, I rowed toward town another five pulls and shipped the oars. It *felt* like the middle of the lake, but I didn't know; it was dark. I picked up the basketball, my old Voit. I'd scored layups on ten driveways in four states with this ball. I felt the ball in my hands. It was a little flat, but I mounted it on my fingertips for the shot, feeling the old worn nubble, and sent it up in a perfect arc, rocking the old wooden boat a bit more than I meant to. I grabbed the gunwales to keep from going in the dark water myself, and I heard the sarisfying *bip*! of the ball's splash.

The sperm's journey is the equivalent of a three-and-a-half-mile swim, so I was going to have to swim from the town beach over to the boathouse and then head for the middle. I rowed back. I pulled the heavy boat up on the sand, dragging it well clear of the water, and I undressed, putting my clothing over the bow. Then I curled onto the cool sand and tried to grow quiet. I was too excited. I could feel, smell, sense the whole round lake lying beside me, and somewhere in the middle, the basketball. I squeezed my eyes shut in joy. This is it. I could feel a warmth in my shoulders and in the backs of my legs; this was really working.

But I'd left nothing to chance. Tomorrow, the garlic would arrive, and I'd pick up the jade. I had ordered the chickens and the birdseed and the rice. I'd become part of a process that had me in its sweep, and in a second, I was on my feet, yipping like a monkey as I rushed in four long strides right into the warm waters of Lake Mugacook.

The medium of the water enveloped, moved me. I was flying, floating, gliding. The trees along the water's edge drifted by as if the lake were quietly turning for me, taking me with it. I closed my eyes as I swam for minutes at a time. By the time I took my first real breath—or so it seemed—I looked up and saw the square white face of the boathouse smiling at me. Behind me, in the middle of this huge lake, the deepest lake in Connecticut, was a basketball. I turned, kicking hard, headed right for it. I imagined the other millions of sperm swimming behind me, wandering, loitering, taking the wrong turn into Cookson Swamp or Succor Brook, drowning in the acid at the top of the vagina, their tails being eaten by antibodies.

I swam for a long time. It became real swimmimg, my arms

finally heavier than the water, and I could hear myself breathing, blowing water out. It was a big lake. When I crawled to where the middle might have been, I sighted the church spire, a lighted sliver over the town. I turned to line up with Ballowells' lights.

There were no lights.

I stood in a treadwater position and swiveled. No lights. Ballowells had gone to bed. Ballowells had turned out every one of their seventy thousand lights and they had gone to bed. I had no idea where I was. For a while I was under the water, which I did know, and I came up several times saying the word "Okay!" spitting like a seal. Across the lake I could still see the white line of the church spire. It was a mile and a quarter to the rowboat, then through the grove, down the pond road a half mile, across Route 43, and up the steps into the church. My knees ached like burning rubber.

I was under, then way under, and then up for air. Each time I cracked the surface my "Okay!" had more water in it, and finally I couldn't even hear the word. This was not a hospitable environment. I went into my drown-proofing moves, but I kept going down too far and had to kick to mouth air. Something touched my toe, something small, but it was enough. I panicked. The antibodies were eating my tail. In a frenzy of side straddle hops, side strokes, leaping waves, I called "Whoa!" and went down.

The water played a lugubrious synthesizer tone in my ears as I fell freely through the thermoclimes past two, three zones of colder water. Small hot squiggles crawled across the inside of my closed eyes. I was swaying back and forth wonderfully. It was like the time I was playing one on one with Billy Wellner at his house. We were playing around his pickup and I perfected a shot where I would drive around the rear of the truck and then lean back into the fence and throw a set shot up off the board and through the hoop. I made the shot nine times in a row and beat Billy 22–2. All he could say was, "You're wrecking the fence."

Then.

Then I touched the basketball, and it was in one hand, then both hands, and my knees closed around it too, as we bobbed past forty-six million stars in outer space.

THE voice behind the flashlight said, "Get up." It was our constable, Gill Manwaring, I could tell, and he was trying to sound real tough. Story herself had hired Gill as constable.

"You better get up, fella."

I lay still, wrapped around the ball, in the same fetal position in which I must have washed upon this shore. He hadn't recognized me. His boot ran up under my kidney. "Up!"

In a voice I recognized as Raymond Burr's, I said, "Hey, Gill." I rose, not unlike a cow would, a piece at a time, and looked into the flashlight. "What time is it?"

"Dan?"

"Yeah." I stood facing him, holding the ball nonchalantly in front of my private parts. He lowered the light and I came to understand there was a personage standing behind Gill.

"You all right?"

"Yeah," I said. "Late night swim got away from me. Can you take me around to my boat? It's at the grove." My eyes adjusted by steady, painful degrees in the starlight, and I could see that this was the three acre front lea of the Ballowells', and that Annette Ballowell was backing steadily toward her dark and significant mansion.

It wasn't until I sat my bare ass on the seat of Gill's Rover that I lifted the ball onto my lap and saw the disturbing and exciting truth: it wasn't the same ball. It wasn't my ball at all.

## S E V E N

*THE* next morning when I removed the thermometer from Story's mouth, she looked up at me. "It's the deep end you're over, isn't it."

I read the thermometer with new intensity. "Ninety-seven point seven."

"Why don't you just paint household objects until it takes. You'll get it. You'll see it again. School will be out this week, and you can just take some time."

"I'm going to do that. I'll be all right." I nodded and heard the angry little tides inside my ears. "I'm going to paint everything."

When Story left for Town Hall, I burst into action. I didn't have class until four, so I ran to the studio barelegged in my Sears robe and stretched three canvases, 60 by 60, my shrunken hands atremble. I could feel the heat. I was in motion; I couldn't do it fast enough. I had one palette wet under cellophane and without changing it a bit, I started in.

The volleyball that had saved my life in the confidential waters of Lake Mugacook ten hours before was a Sportcraft Professional Model manufactured in New Castle, Pennsylvania. In postal blue magic marker script along one seam was the name: Allen. Luther Allen was a retired broker who clipped coupons on his lakefront property in town. His children and grandchildren came up from New York and New Haven on weekends.

On the first canvas, I broadbrushed the curve of one side in vermilion. I had to hold my head cocked a certain way as the lakewater gurgled up and down my eustachian tubes. Many times when I changed positions, water ran out of my ears. I worked fast because I figured I had two hours tops before Story ran into Gill Manwaring and I'd get a phone call. If I could grab a secure start on three canvases, it might testify to my equilibrium. But as my hands moved across the paintings, working all three in one stroke, then one for twenty minutes, I wondered. They didn't look like volleyballs as we know them.

So many times the magic in painting transpires in the twelve inches between the palette and the canvas, and your head, hand, or heart better get out of the way. I felt that warmth in my arms now, and I tried to proceed with caution or reason or passionless purpose, but I might as well not have been there. This was not the way I used to paint. I ran from the studio several times, whenever my neck would get too sore, and I dressed a piece at a time, retrieved the hammer, all my roofing nails, the butcher knife. My garlic was arriving at noon.

When the phone did ring, Story simply said, "What's going on?"

"Story, I've got a start on three good pieces. Can I call you back?"

"Dan, what's this with Gill?"

"Don't worry. Don't worry. Don't worry. I'll tell you later. All about it. I gotta go." And I did go. I found myself an hour later in the studio, one canvas finished, the others running to a close. The first looked like nothing, like a rose moon in a blue blanket, I don't know, but God it thrilled me! Some of the edges floated like folded velvet; I'd never done that before. I'd never seen it done before! This was no landscape that I knew. The whole time I'd been in the studio, I'd only had two thoughts. One was simply a picture of Story's face as she hung up the phone: that worry. The other was so profound it powered me through the day. I wanted, more than anything, for my children and grand-children to come visit and play volleyball on the lawn. The picture made sense and gave reason to everything in my life.

The garlic man, not a farmer but Cummings from the Food

Center, had to come all the way through the house and he startled me, appearing at the studio door. I hadn't heard him for all the water in my ears.

Cummings was also the butcher, and as he stood at my studio doorway in his bloody apron, he seemed one of the Fates come to abbreviate me at last.

"I've got your garlic," he said, and the first glorious strains of the herb drifted my way.

"Good!" I must have said it a little too loudly as Mr. Cummings stepped back and raised his hands in self-defense. To assure him that I meant no harm, I placed my brush and palette aside and asked him in to see what I was doing. He folded his arms over his apron and browsed my canvases, nodding steadily. The spectacle of the three huge canvases, flashed and spiraled with those strange colors, and the volleyball sitting on the table behind them seemed to confuse Mr. Cummings, but his nodding quickened. His assessment was only "Yep," followed by seven or eight small "Yep, yep, yeps." It didn't strike me until we had unloaded two hundred pounds of garlic onto the front lawn, that Mr. Cumming's yepping had been identical to the sad and final pronouncements of a doctor whose suspicions have been confirmed.

When he left, I didn't hesitate. I took up my hammer and jammed my pockets with the short galvanized roofing nails, and wondered why the opinion of one of the most prominent village tradesmen didn't bother me; why in fact, I took his incredulity as encouragement; why, in fact, I felt absolutely encouraged by everything in the world: the flat noon light, the impending thundershower, Mudd Miller's black Honda motorcycle leaking oil on his driveway across the street. Oh, I just breathed it all in and began tacking the garlic to my own sweet home.

I framed all the doors in garlands first, in case there wasn't enough garlic, tapping the nails through the center of each bulb, spacing them three fingers apart. Then I ringed the windows, the basement windows, and the storm cellar door. The oil each clove gave its nail slathered down my wrists to the elbows, but after twenty minutes, I couldn't smell a thing. It all gave our house a fuzzy, gingerbread look, not unbecoming and kind of festive. By the time I finished, I was high, high with a new taut certainty that I was unquestionably on the right track, and high with a sort of major garlic sinus dilation. My eyes felt poached.

I ran to the studio to retrieve my car keys, but was again arrested by the three paintings and worked for a furious moment on the third. This "volleyball" was becoming more elongated than the other two and looked like, I'll say for now, a rose setting sun in a green and ocher sky. But something told me that when I looked into the canvas I wasn't looking all the way to the horizon. Something was trying to get out; I love that sense. When the phone rang, I came to and strode out to my old Buick. I sat still in the driver's seat for a moment, listening to the phone ringing. It sounded like a vague, intermittent alert for the future going off in garlic house.

In my book, *Life Before Science*, it said:

Garlic and garlic substitutes were often used by tribes in Africa, Asia, Austrailia, and England to heat a childless domecile. The huts were festooned with fresh garlic once a month, and the man and the woman wore garlic in various forms sewn into a garment or on a string around the neck, or crushed into the hair. Some tribes were known to use a garlic mattress, which was rumored to have never failed. In many societies the smell of garlic was synonymous with fecundity.

71

*E I G H T*

*Y O U* lay yourself open to attack by a powerful creeping chagrin
if you drive miles away from home one fine afternoon, as I did,
guided only by your overwhelming desire to have children and
by a lurid, illustrated half-page advertisement from the back pages
of the scurrilous local shopper *The Twilight Want Ads*. Just the
tabloid illustration mocked me: a crude wood block print fea-
turing, or so it said, Mrs. Argyle, "Gypsy Wizardress, Alchemist,
Seer, and Tax Advisor," her face seemingly radiating small light-
ning rays of power and—what I took to be—understanding.

So I set my mouth against the thorough feeling that I was a
fool, and I followed the directions Mrs. Argyle had given me
over the telephone, driving toward the village of Boughton, where
I had never been.

The interview that followed, in the woody turnout three point
four miles from Boughton, with Mrs. Argyle, is still a mystery
to me. Her rusty Ford van was there along with the two jade
talismans hanging from the rearview mirror. I stood around for
a while, trying to look innocent, and then finally I put two
hundred dollars on the seat, as I'd been instructed in our call,
took the necklaces, and left.

Driving home was a different matter. Cruising the rural roads
in Connecticut after twilight in the early summer, past farmers'
fields and the little roadhouses, their pink Miller Beer signs just
beginning to glow in the new darkness, with two *guaranteed* jade
talismans in my pocket, I began to swell with confidence and
good cheer. I sang songs that I made up (with gestures) and
grinned like an idiot. I never saw Mrs. Argyle at all. I motored
toward Bigville, my mouth full of song, the jade glowing at my
side.

At garlic headquarters, my house, Story was waiting. I could see my sweet mayor and Ruth Wellner, my favorite county attorney, having Piels Light on the rocks with a twist in the living room. Piels beer is the only thing Story drinks, always on ice with a twist, and I had come to see the brown bottles with their cadmium orange labels as little symbols of pleasure and ease, perhaps celebration. But this time as I walked through the kitchen and saw the bottles standing on the counter, I don't know, I was worried. Our normal life was amazing; why did I want to tamper with it? But then I thought: okay, if this is what I have to do to create another human being, to have a son or daughter with whom to play catch and Scrabble, and to show Picasso and Chagall, and to teach how to fish and to cook a good garlic sauce for spaghetti squash, someone to send to the fridge for another beer and who will chase his sister through the house with a pair of scissors and to lend the car keys to and to ground for two weeks for being late for some ridiculous curfew and to spend two hundred thousand dollars on and to leave all my stuff to, my collection of Monster Magazines, my hand-tied flies, my railroad watch, though it is broken, and someone to fake-right, go-left past for the hoop, and to paint a thousand versions of before I die, then okay, I'll do it. I entered the living room.

Ruth Wellner gave me the hardest ride with her eyeballs I'd ever had. "Hi, everybody!" I said. "How's the township?"

Story smiled at me, which is great about her. She always smiles at me at first. Then, of course, she said, "What's going *on*, Dan?" I thought for a moment that she had read my mind or had seen the two lumps of jade in my pocket, but then she went on: "What have you done to the house?"

"Oh! Yeah." I hadn't thought of an answer, especially in front of the county attorney. "It's a conceptual piece I'm trying."

"Garlic?"

"This one's garlic." I said, wishing I'd grabbed a beer. "It's been done with apples." I nodded, believing what I'd said myself. "It's only a temporary piece," I explained, waving my hands as a kind of truce. Ruth leaned back and shook her head imperceptibly, a subtle gesture they all learn in law school which means: "I don't believe a word of it, you lying bastard." But Story smiled at me again, a new smile this time, the ancient smile of women who know their men.

"You missed your class, you know."

"Oh, sure," I said affirmatively. "Sure, sure. That's wonderful." And it was wonderful in my crazy head. I could see my students waiting for the keys to unlock their lockers, grumbling and then drifting away. Mary Ann Buxton would have drifted right to the department chairman's office to offer him most of an earful, but it was wonderful. I smiled. I put my hand over the two charms in my pocket and I realized that I was moving through the most centered and affirmative period of my life. And though I couldn't see them all clearly, there were still things to do.

## N I N E

IN the morning, I placed the thermometer in Story's mouth and sang three minutes from the theme song of *High Noon*, making the "Do not forsake me, oh my darling!" really mournful, and then read the little gauge: "Ninety-seven point nine. Or ninety-eight flat, I can't tell."

I felt an almost impossible intensity, an anticipation that ran me with chills. All my magic was aligned for tonight, all my preparations.

"You're in a . . . mood," Story said cautiously, giving me an odd side glance.

"Good night's sleep," I said trying to suddenly appear mature. I stood and the song rose into my throat. "On this our we-e-edding day-ay!" I sang and headed for the bathroom.

In the shower steam rose around me rife with garlic, the very smell of babies hovering in the air. There was nothing wrong with us. Tonight was the night.

Story came into the bathroom just in time to hear the best rhyme in my song:

> "He'd made a vow while in state prison,
> Vow'd it'd be my life or his'n!"

"Oh, this garlic!" she yelled. "This garlic has got to go!"

"Tomorrow," I answered. "Just one more day."

"You know what Ruth thinks?"

"That she could get me off with insanity?"

"That you're having an affair."

I poked my head outside the shower curtain and stared at Story. She was naked, brushing her teeth, and the way she bent to the sink burned across my heart. "What?"

Story tapped her brush and looked up. Such a smile. "You're not having an affair. You've got your secrets, but you're not having an affair."

Before Story left for the office, I grabbed her lapels and said, "Listen, try this: get the township business out of your head, okay? If you have to, delegate some authority, make a new committee, but get it out of your head. And Story."

"Yes, sir?"

"Come home alone. No Ruthless Ruth. No complicated preoccupations. Just you. Seven o'clock."

"Is there something I should know, Dan?"

I showed her my palms and waved one up at the garlic doorway fringe. "You know it all already. I'll see you at seven."

She gave me a funny, get-well-soon look, and I thought what it must be like for the mayor to be married to a wizard-master of the dark and light arts, but I also thought: *it's worth it*. She'll go and worry about me for thirty-five minutes, until township troubles hit the fan, and it's worth it.

After Story had left, I ran up to the campus for my ten o'clock life class, arriving just in time to let Tim, our model, in early. An irrepressible townie, he sits for the group bareassed in a buckskin jockstrap on a wooden stool, one knee drawn up to his chest, his heel on the stool seat. As he passed by me to go change clothes, he said: "One more time! Tomorrow I'm in Virginia Beach, and," he pointed at me and smirked, "art class is history."

I had forgotten: it was the last day of school. I was surprised and for the first time in weeks, time became real. My students filed in around me, and I had to smile; this was certainly a waking dream, but a good dream.

Mary Ann Buxton was waiting for me as I drifted among the easels. Seated directly behind Tim, she had drawn an incredibly precise version of the stool and had skipped up and drawn his shoulder axis and neck.

"Where were you yesterday?" she said. "The studio class, all nine of us, waited forty-five minutes. Is this what we pay tuition for?"

I wanted to say: Truce; it's the last day of school. Cease further hostilities. But I did say: "I'm sorry, Mary Ann; I was away." Before she could start again, I interrupted her with this whisper: "Mary Ann. What's he going to sit on?" I pointed to the blank space on her paper where his ass should have been. "Don't be shy," I said. "This is art." I couldn't stop myself; I winked. "Go ahead, really."

I was in a daze the whole hour. The volleyball at home. I couldn't see a thing but the ball and the three paintings emerging in my mind. I wandered the studio muttering, "Good, good," to everybody, even Mary Ann Buxton and her feathered fluffy version of Tim's posterior. It was a tangible relief when Tim himself stood up, stretched, and said, "Okay. That's my twenty bucks. Anybody looking now pays overtime."

Oh, Bigville! You sweet township! What I did the rest of the day was seen through eyes blurred by heat and vision. I shook hands with my fine young painters and headed out, running across campus, gathering a hundred stares in my wake. If any dean had been looking out the window, I would have received a letter.

At home, I retrieved the ten-pound bag of rice and the fifty pounds of birdseed from the basement and spread them in a blinding flurry of thrown handfuls across the backyard, and incidentally my hair, the roof, and the raingutters.

I went to see Mr. Cummings at the Food Center and he had my two chickens, that is, their innards, and he handed me the plastic pail without a look, my eccentricity gone ordinary in his eyes. At home, crackling across the birdseed and rice, I tossed gloopy handfuls of the intestines, etcetera, around the yard. I stripped off my shirt and made circles on my belly with the blood. I bent and tried to read the throws. I'm not sure what they said, but they looked authentic. I went into the basement and drew on the furnace room walls with charcoal briquets: sperm entering the egg, wiggling tails, hash marks of excitement, seven stars, the blistered moon. When I came back upstairs, blinking into the light, I saw Buster and Sadie, Mudd Miller's two dogs, rolling on their backs in the chicken guts. It dismayed me at first until I remembered that Sadie had already thrown three healthy litters of five puppies each, and I debated whether to go out and writhe around with them for a while.

The doorbell rang, and it turned out to be Mary Ann Buxton, in her traveling clothes, her little Volvo packed to the windows, still running on the driveway. She looked at me in a three-part glance: my charcoaled face, my bloody belly, and then, stepping back slowly, the aboriginal whole. There was nothing I could do.

"Hello," I said.

"Mr. Baldwin," she said finally. "Thank you for the help and encouragement in art this year. I've learned a lot. It was one of my favorite classes, and in appreciation, I brought you this little present."

It was a prepared speech or she wouldn't have gotten through it, and she managed a "Thank you and good-bye," handing me something and backing down the stairs with a look of frenzied relief on her face. She was glad to have left the car running.

I looked in my hand. It was her painting of the four birches near the Dean's garden. My eyes burned inexplicably, and I went back into the house and sat on the floor in the hallway for a moment. Mary Ann Buxton had squatted outdoors for three days frowning at this canvas, chewing her lip, and it was a good painting, two steps beyond representational. I looked at it for five minutes, as if I was counting the strokes. Those damn trees. I love those trees.

In my studio, my three paintings rose to me like live things. I buried my heart into the third and final canvas. I didn't look up again until I heard Mudd Miller on his porch calling the names of his children, the ones he could remember. Oh, it was a bellow full of love! I looked at myself, covered with blood and paint and charcoal, my face a savage smear in the mirror. "Oh, Bigville," I moaned aloud. "It's all going to work."

I showered and began to cool down. I called the office and Ruth Wellner said the meeting would go another hour. I stood in the dining room looking out through a window ringed by garlic at my yard littered with chicken waste, rice, and birdseed, and I had the momentary thought: "You fool, you've ruined your own home." But it was a fleeting doubt and to quash it, I did an errand. I drove the Sportcraft volleyball over to Luther Allen's and left it with the groundskeeper.

Story did not arrive home until after ten. I had roamed the house for a while, cruising my new paintings with a hot, fond confusion. I liked them even if I didn't know what they were. Finally I settled in the living room with Mary Ann Buxton's four birches propped against the mantel where I could see them, and *Life Before Science* on my lap. In the new darkness, the volume put my legs to sleep and I followed soon thereafter. It was a heavy book.

I was dreaming of Dr. Binderwitz scolding me, pointing his unwashed finger in my face, when Story woke me, bumping me softly with her leg. "Hey," she said. "Did you eat?"

I checked my watch: ten-thirty. "What happened?"

"Want some chicken?" she said. "I brought you some chicken."

So we ate cold chicken and drank Piels Light on the rocks at the kitchen table like two characters in a good short novel while I woke up and Story gave me the details of the meeting.

As Story told me the tale, she laughed and ate chicken and we drank cold beer, and the moment in the kitchen light reminded me in a primal way of why and how much I loved her.

"I'm painting again," I said.

"I knew you would." She reached and took my forearm.

"Wait here," I told her, and I rose and fetched my two jade friends from the bureau. I put one around her neck and one around my own. Chin down, Story examined her necklace.

"You need to wear it tonight, while we . . ."

"Interact sexually?"

I nodded.

"Well, you are dear, aren't you," she said. "Confused, but dear."

"Can you get the township out of your head long enough to conceive a baby?"

"Come here," she said. "Come get me."


WE didn't make it to the bedroom. She started playing Eva Marie Saint in *On the Waterfront* and sliding down the hall doorframe, her arms around my neck, and by the time we were on our knees, no one was playing anymore, or rather, now we were playing in earnest. Several times we stopped and shifted to gain leg room, and we rolled, twice, three times, I don't know, but then we were under the piano in a pane of moonlight, and I don't know, her flesh, her breath, I was on my back and I could see the round moon just like an egg sliding down the blue-black tube of the sky. We were gathering the pieces as she held me, three hundred million coiled swimmers in a garlic sea, and in a rush that grabbed my throat like a fist, they were flying.

The first thing I saw when I took my mouth from Story's was the grouping of my three fingers over her white shoulder, those three bald men come to greet us, but then as my eyes rinsed once more I saw them again and this is when I saw it all: they weren't three old men at all, but three babies I had seen somewhere before. My eyes filled. Three babies. I had painted these guys for the last week, each on a canvas of his own.

Story reached her arm around my neck and turned on her side. "Are you going to get us a blanket?" she said. "Or shall we go to bed?"

I got her the quilt. In my study the only light came from the children. Not one: three. I painted until blue dawn and they focused like photographs: three babies. From my window I could see the sun about to burst over Mugacook Mountain; the trees stood out in chromosomal pairs. My heart was swimming. I could see the children, do you see? In her arms. One. Two. Three.

# II

# BIGFOOT STOLE
# MY WIFE

*THE* problem is credibility.

The problem, as I'm finding out over the last few weeks, is basic credibility. A lot of people look at me and say, sure Rick, Bigfoot stole your wife. It makes me sad to see it, the look of disbelief in each person's eye. Trudy's disappearance makes me sad, too, and I'm sick in my heart about where she may be and how he's treating her, what they do all day, if she's getting enough to eat. I believe he's being good to her—I mean I feel it—and I'm going to keep hoping to see her again, but it is my belief that I probably won't.

In the two and a half years we were married, I often had the feeling that I would come home from the track and something would be funny. Oh, she'd say things: *One of these days I'm not going to be here when you get home*, things like that, things like everybody says. How stupid of me not to see them as omens. When I'd get out of bed in the early afternoon, I'd stand right here at this sink and I could see her working in her garden in her cut-off Levis and bikini top, weeding, planting, watering. I mean it was obvious. I was too busy thinking about the races, weighing the odds, checking the jockey roster to see what I now know: he was watching her too. He'd probably been watching her all summer.

So, in a way it was my fault. But what could I have done? Bigfoot steals your wife. I mean: even if you're home, it's going to be a mess. He's big and not well trained.

When I came home it was about eleven-thirty. The lights were on, which really wasn't anything new, but in the ordinary mess of the place, there was a little difference, signs of a struggle. There was a spilled Dr. Pepper on the counter and the fridge was open. But there was something else, something that made me sick. The smell. The smell of Bigfoot. It was hideous. It was . . . the guy is not clean.

Half of Trudy's clothes are gone, not all of them, and there is no note. Well, I know what it is. It's just about midnight there in the kitchen which smells like some part of hell. I close the fridge door. It's the saddest thing I've ever done. There's a picture of Trudy and me leaning against her Toyota taped to the fridge door. It was taken last summer. There's Trudy in her bikini top, her belly brown as a bean. She looks like a kid. She was a kid I guess, twenty-six. The two times she went to the track with me everybody looked at me like how'd I rate her. But she didn't really care for the races. She cared about her garden and Chinese cooking and Buster, her collie, who I guess Bigfoot stole too. Or ate. Buster isn't in the picture, he was nagging my nephew Chuck who took the photo. Anyway I close the fridge door and it's like part of my life closed. Bigfoot steals your wife and you're in for some changes.

You come home from the track having missed the Daily Double by a neck, and when you enter the home you are paying for and in which you and your wife and your wife's collie live, and your wife and her collie are gone as is some of her clothing, there is nothing to believe. Bigfoot stole her. It's a fact. What I should I do, ignore it? Chuck came down and said something like well if Bigfoot stole her why'd they take the Celica? Christ, what a cynic! Have you ever read anything about Bigfoot not being able to drive? He'd be cramped in there, but I'm sure he could manage.

I don't really care if people believe me or not. Would that change anything? Would that bring Trudy back here? Pull the weeds in her garden?

As I think about it, no one believes anything anymore. Give me one example of someone *believing* one thing. I dare you. After that we get into this credibility thing. No one believes me. I myself can't believe all the suspicion and cynicism there is in today's world. Even at the races, some character next to me will poke over at my tip sheet and ask me if I believe that stuff. If I believe? What is there to believe? The horse's name? What he did the last time out? And I look back at this guy, too cheap to go two bucks on the program, and I say: it's history. It is historical fact here. Believe. Huh. Here's a fact: I believe everything.

Credibility.

When I was thirteen years old, my mother's trailer was washed away in the flooding waters of the Harley River and swept thirty-one miles, ending right side up and nearly dead level just outside Mercy, in fact in the old weed-eaten parking lot for the abandoned potash plant. I know this to be true because I was inside the trailer the whole time with my pal, Nuggy Reinecker, who found the experience more life-changing than I did.

Now who's going to believe this story? I mean, besides me, because I was there. People are going to say, come on, thirty-one miles? Don't you mean thirty-one feet?

We had gone in out of the rain after school to check out a magazine that belonged to my mother's boyfriend. It was a copy of *Dude*, and there was a fold-out page I will never forget of a girl lying on the beach on her back. It was a color photograph. The girl was a little pale, I mean, this was probably her first day out in the sun, and she had no clothing on. So it was good, but what made it great was that they had made her a little bathing suit out of sand. Somebody had spilled a little sand just right, here and there, and the sand was this incredible gold color, and it made her look so absolutely naked it wanted to put your eyes out.

Nuggy and I knew there was flood danger in Griggs; we'd had a flood every year almost and it had been raining for five days on and off, but when the trailer bucked the first time, we thought it was my mother come home to catch us in the dirty book. Nuggy shoved the magazine under the bed and I ran out to check the door. It only took me a second and I hollered back *Hey no sweat, no one's here*, but by the time I returned to see what other poses they'd had this beautiful woman commit, Nuggy already had his pants to his ankles and was involved in what we knew was a sin.

If it hadn't been the timing of the first wave with this act of his, Nuggy might have gone on to live what the rest of us call a normal life. But the Harley had crested and the head wave, which they estimated to be three feet minimum, unmoored the trailer with a push that knocked me over the sofa, and threw Nuggy, already entangled in his trousers, clear across the bedroom.

I watched the village of Griggs as we sailed through. Some of the village, the Exxon Station, part of it at least, and the carwash, which folded up right away, tried to come along with us, and I saw the front of Painters' Mercantile, the old porch and signboard, on and off all day.

You can believe this: it was not a smooth ride. We'd rip along for ten seconds, dropping and growling over rocks, and rumbling over tree stumps, and then wham! the front end of the trailer would lodge against a rock or something that could stop it, and whoa! we'd wheel around sharp as a carnival ride, worse really, because the furniture would be thrown against the far side and us with it, sometimes we'd end up in a chair and sometimes the chair would sit on us. My mother had about four thousand knick-knacks in five big box shelves, and they gave us trouble for the first two or three miles, flying by like artillery, left, right, some small glass snail hits you in the face, later in the back, but that stuff all finally settled in the foot and then two feet of water which we took on.

We only slowed down once and it was the worst. In the railroad flats I thought we had stopped and I let go of the door I was hugging and tried to stand up and then swish, another rush sent us right along. We rammed along all day it seemed, but when we finally washed up in Mercy and the sheriff's cousin pulled open the door and got swept back to his car by water and quite a few of those knickknacks, just over an hour had passed. We had averaged, they figured later, about thirty-two miles an hour, reaching speeds of up to fifty at Lime Falls and the Willows. I was okay and walked out bruised and well washed, but when the sheriff's cousin pulled Nuggy out, he looked genuinely hurt.

"For godsakes," I remember the sheriff's cousin saying, "The damn flood knocked this boy's pants off!" But Nuggy wasn't talking. In fact, he never hardly talked to me again in the two years he stayed at the Regional School. I heard later, and I believe it, that he joined the monastery over in Malcolm County.

My mother, because she didn't have the funds to haul our rig back to Griggs, worried for a while, but then the mayor arranged to let us stay out where we were. So after my long ride in a trailer down the flooded Harley River with my friend Nuggy Reinecker, I grew up in a parking lot outside of Mercy, and to tell you the truth, it wasn't too bad, even though our trailer never did smell straight again.

Now you can believe all that. People are always saying: don't believe everything you read, or everything you hear. And I'm here to tell you. Believe it. Everything. Everything you read. Everything you hear. Believe your eyes. Your ears. Believe the small hairs on the back of your neck. Believe all of history, and all of the versions of history, and all the predictions for the future. Believe every weather forecast. Believe in God, the afterlife, unicorns, showers on Tuesday. Everything has happened. Everything is possible.

I come home from the track to find the cupboard bare. Trudy is not home. The place smells funny: hairy. It's a fact and I know it as a fact: Bigfoot has been in my house.

Bigfoot stole *my* wife.

She's gone.

Believe it.

I gotta believe it.

# I AM BIGFOOT

*THAT'S* fine. I'm ready.

I am Bigfoot. The Bigfoot. You've been hearing about me for some time now, seeing artists' renderings, and perhaps a phony photograph or two. I should say right here that an artist's rendering is one thing, but some trumped-up photograph is entirely another. The one that really makes me sick purports to show me standing in a stream in Northern California. Let me tell you something: Bigfoot never gets his feet wet. And I've only been to Northern California once, long enough to check out Redding and Eureka, both too quiet for the kind of guy I am.

Anyway, all week long, people (the people I contacted) have been wondering why I finally have gone public. A couple thought it was because I was angry at that last headline, remember: "Jackie O. Slays Bigfoot." No, I'm not angry. You can't go around and correct everybody who slanders you. (Hey, I'm not dead, and I only saw Jacqueline Onasssis once, at about four hundred yards. She was on a horse.) And as for libel, what should I do, go up to Rockefeller Center and hire a lawyer? Please. Spare me. You can quote me on this: Bigfoot is not interested in legal action.

*"THEN,* why?" they say. "Why climb out of the woods and go through the trouble of 'meeting the press,' so to speak? (Well,

first of all, I don't live in the woods *year round*, which is a popular misconception of my life-style. Sure, I like the woods, but I need action too. I've had some of my happiest times in the median of the Baltimore Belt-route, the orchards of Arizona and Florida, and I spent nearly five years in the corn country just outside St. Louis. So, it's not just the woods, okay?)

*WHY* I came forward at this time concerns the truest thing I ever read about myself in the papers. The headline read "Bigfoot Stole My Wife," and it was right on the money. But beneath it was the real story: "Anguished Husband's Cry." Now I read the article, every word. Twice. It was poorly written, but it was all true. I stole the guy's wife. She wasn't the first and she wasn't the last. But when I went back and read that "anguished husband," it got me a little. I've been, as you probably have read, in all fifty states and eleven foreign countries. (I have never been to Tibet, in case you're wondering. That is some other guy, maybe the same one who was crossing that stream in Northern California.) *And,* in each place I've been, there's a woman. Come on, who is surprised by that? I don't always steal them, in fact, I never *steal* them, but I do *call them away*, and they come with me. I know my powers and I use my powers. And when I call a woman, she comes.

*SO, HERE I AM.* It's kind of a confession, I guess; kind of a warning. I've been around; I've been all over the world (except Tibet! I don't know if that guy is interested in women or not.) And I've seen thousands of women standing at their kitchen windows, their stare in the mid-afternoon goes a thousand miles; I've seen thousands of women, dressed to the nines, strolling the cosmetic counters in Saks and I. Magnin, wondering why their lives aren't like movies; thousands of women shuffling in the soft twilight of malls, headed for the Orange Julius stand, not really there, just biding time until things get lovely.

And things get lovely when I call. I cannot count them all, I cannot list the things these women are doing while their husbands are out there in another world, but one by one I'm meeting them on my terms. I am Bigfoot. I am not from Tibet. I go from village to town to city to village. At present, I am watching your wife. That's why I am here tonight. To tell you, fairly, man to man, I suppose, I am watching your wife and I know for a fact, that when I call, she'll come.

# MADAME ZELENA
# FINALLY
# COMES CLEAN

*THE* first thing I ever saw in the future was a whale. I mean I saw a beautiful gray whale at close range. I didn't know what it was, but I've seen it twice since, and it's still in the future but now I know what it means.

You probably know me best as Madame Zelena from the column I used to write, "Zodiac Tomorrow," for *Realms of Twilight Tabloid News of the World*. That's not my real name. My real name is Janet Wigg, but that isn't a real great name for a clairvoyant so I was Madame Zelena for three years, and if you were keeping track you know my record there in the annual forecasts was 93 percent, which is good in any league.

People want to know about the future. Isn't that funny? Because the truth is that the real mystery is the past. Not the prehistoric past, the unrecorded history of our race, our ancestors, but the real mysterious past. Last week. What happened last week? What happened last October? What happened in the Spring of 1979? What happened yesterday? We can all see the future. You know where you'll be tomorrow at eleven A.M.. Tomorrow night. A week from Saturday. We can all see that; it's just the future, but where have we been?

As a child I didn't know I could see the future. I thought I had a lot of dreams like any kid, but every once in a while we'd be in the car and I'd know that around the next corner about halfway down the block there'd be a dog, a black dog jumping around with two kids, two boys in cut-off Levis tossing a brown tennis ball back and forth. For a while I thought nothing of it, I thought maybe I had been down that street before, but then it started happening everywhere.

One time my mother and my stepfather, Mickey, and I drove from Reno where he was a dealer, up over Tahoe and down to Sacramento. I knew everything, even how the birds would cross the highway ahead of us, six long birds going real slow. It was the birds, more than the highway signs (which I'd read before they appeared), that woke me to this little power of mine. I'd see a sign, "Rudy's Motel, Better Bed and Bath, 40 miles," aloud and then the sign would appear. Mickey said, "We're going to get this girl's eyes checked." I looked at him driving our Datsun, his plaid shirt making him look almost normal, and I saw him in prison, which is where he was in a year for some cheap casino scam. The day he was arrested I went down to J.B.'s where my mother was a waitress (I must have been about seven by then) and I looked at her through the windows, watched her set coffee in front of all those people, but I couldn't see her at all. The reason was that she wasn't going anywhere. She's still there.

As I grew up I couldn't always see things, the things that were going to happen. The power, or whatever you want to call it, was a lot like the way anybody sees things. We just don't always see. When was the last time you looked at a tree—or a cloud? But other times I would be so awake or wired with fatigue that things would jump out at me. I could see the car in front of me at a traffic light upside down in three weeks in a junkyard. I could see my mother watching a new T.V., I could see myself in the backseat of some hoodlum's Pontiac, being pressed into next week, my neck against the door in a posture I still associate somehow with pleasure.

But I knew, in flashes over the years, that I would eventually marry a lovely man. I'm a patient person. When you can see the future, even some of it, why not be?

I didn't go to college, though I could have and I'd have done as well as I did in high school in Reno; I knew what was on the tests three weeks beforehand. The only B I got was in health where I knew the exam, sure, but the day Miss Evers handed it out, she touched my hand and I saw her drowning on a river trip that summer. Her face, blue and swollen, rolled before me the whole hour. I never finished the test.

And since then, for more or less the same reason, I haven't finished much. I became a nurse's aide at Good Samaritan right in Reno and it wasn't such a bad job because about half the people I nursed were going to get better, which is a higher average than you meet on the streets. Some guy would lie there rattling for a week, that is when he wasn't sweating blood, but I could see him in two months at the drive-in window at McDonalds ordering a quarter pounder with cheese and fries and it made it all easier, a possible job. Then I met the intern and it was like seeing his face again. His name was Allen Wigg, and as soon as I met him I saw the other thing, the other person, Irene, my daughter, so I bore down and put Allen through his internship while I swelled up big as a whale.

During my pregnancy I couldn't see a thing. It was wonderful. My work at the hospital took on a day-to-day quality that I loved. Things got dirty, I washed them. Something would drop on the floor, I would clean it up. It was cause and effect, no thick vertigo full of sad cinema. How I loved those slow days, each separate from the other, the only continuum my stomach filling with my daughter Irene.

The day she was born I passed out for thirty-six hours during which I saw the rest. I even saw this night, tonight. I saw it all.

Two weeks after Irene was born, Josie, the nine-year old daughter of the couple who shared our duplex, disappeared. They searched for her for two months before I walked into the police station one day and told them to look a hundred yards below the end of Wymer's old dirt road at the base of Brave Mountain. I'd known about it for five weeks, ever since the mother, Samantha, who everybody called Sam, and who was close as close with me while I was carrying Irene, who taught me the real simple pleasure of gossip and the small satisfaction of folding clothes, Samantha came over, not crying, and she touched my hand as I gave her the coffee and I saw the guy drop the body on the ground. I knew where he was because that was Brave Mountain right behind him. I got scared because it was all starting again, and this time it was serious. I knew what would happen if I went to the police and it did happen, you didn't have to be psychic to see that. But I couldn't let Norm and Samantha go on not knowing where their baby was. I thought of anonymous notes. I thought of anonymous calls, but no. Do you see? A little girl was dead, and you can't stop it. I saw it all.

When the police returned that afternoon it was already in the papers: PSYCHIC FINDS BODY OF MISSING GIRL. Psychic. I've always loved that word. One of the first movies Allen took me to was *Harper*, starring Paul Newman, and he has that line in the roadhouse where he says to the bartender, "You must be physic," meaning "psychic." I must be physic. But it was in the papers.

The next day the press started coming round and that was pretty hard on Allen, who is a kind man and a fine doctor, to have these monkeys in our front yard with cameras and a newborn girl in the house, but the worst was the letters and phone calls. Could I come to Portland to find a man's wife? Could I come to Baton Rouge and find the missing children. Just the letters in my hands started all the strange engines of seeing in my heart.

The guys finally climbed off our lawn, but the mail kept up steady. Every other day I'd get a call, some female voice so full of electricity I'd end up sitting on the floor with the receiver in my lap. She was sure if I'd just come and sit in Terry's room, I could find her baby.

I stopped eating, and in a week I was this old. That was twelve years ago. Late, late at night when I was in bed with Allen, I'd get up and go out on the porch in Reno, Nevada, and just try to see the stars. Do you see? My life was over. I could see it all, and let me say it plain: that is no comfort. You want to see the future? You're welcome to it.

The night I left, I held Irene in my arms. I stood naked in the nursery Allen and I had fixed up together and I held her naked in my naked arms, and when I saw her and what time had in store for her, I set her down, dressed, and left. She's okay. She's going to be an architect. Isn't that wonderful? And Allen's okay. He won't win the Nobel Peace Prize, but he'll have three articles in *The New England Journal of Medicine* soon, two in one issue, and he has a fine woman who lives with him outside of Reno now, his wife, a woman with a garden.

I drifted around Nevada for a while doing honest work, trying not to touch anyone. I went to Arizona for the horse races, but found I couldn't pick a winner, some jockey's miseries would get in my way or sometimes I could only see some old horse standing on a rocky slope in his old age waiting to be fed. So I went back up to Vegas, felt my way around for a while, and found that I could make a lot of money playing craps. I tried to be careful and only slipped up once toward the end of the three months I was banking it away. I got a little sick of the town, sick of my motel on Fremont, and I wanted to send Allen and Irene the money and be done with the West and its vistas, so to speak. I hopped on the hardways one night at the Union Plaza and hit them so cleanly that the pit boss took over the stick and then some folks gathered around, but I didn't care, them calling me "Lady Luck" and following me on the hard eight, the hard ten. I made my last bet under the eyes of the manager—nine hundred on boxcars at thirty to one. I saw them a full minute before all twelve dots rolled fatly up to everybody's eyes. There was a cheer that shut the place down. When the manager handed me the slip for my winnings, he touched my finger and I saw his forehead through the windshield of his Seville off the Searchlight highway in a ditch. Since I'd broken all my rules about using the vision that night anyway, I said to him: "Stop drinking, you're going to kill yourself."

That article was in the paper too, about "Lady Luck," this mystery woman taking forty thousand out of the Plaza, but they didn't have a picture, so I was okay. I sent the clipping and most of the money to Allen. In the note I said, "I'll always love you," because it was true, and because I could see his good face when he read it. So, then I was clear. I just had these terrible eyes, but no one else, no one to hurt or to complicate with hurt the rest of my life.

I used my money staying away from people, traveling first class where you don't have to touch, and staying in the best hotels where you're basically paying for everyone to stay away from you. I didn't want to hand some bellboy a dollar and see him raping his sister. I didn't want time to have its way with me.

In the winter, some years later, I was in Toronto on the third floor of the Toronto Hilton when I saw Anwar Sadat killed. I was in the bathtub taking one of the many baths I took every day, not reading, not listening to the radio, and I saw the stands and the parade and the truck coming.

I got dressed, went down to the bar, and picked up a professor from the University of Ontario who was at a Joyce Carol Oates

Conference and took him to my room for a day and a half until he had to deliver his paper. It was the first sexual experience I had had since Allen, and it was fine in that it filled me with nothing but this professor and the ten million student papers he was going to read poorly the rest of his career, but when he went downstairs to address the multitudes, I turned in the bed and saw the truck, the parade, the stands.

I left Toronto. Do you see? I didn't know what to do.

I worked in a Wendy's in Birmingham, Alabama, for almost a month. What a joke. By then I needed the money, but the people would come to the counter and I'd hand them their order. Talk about fast food. I didn't do it on purpose. I'd turn to them thinking they had already asked for chili and a double cheeseburger with everything on it and a medium-sized Dr. Pepper. I'd hand it to them before they had said a word and I'd say that will be $5.47. I mean, it troubled the customers. The manager put me on the drive-up window, but it was the same there, worse maybe, because I could lean over and see into their cars, and if you want to see people's futures, just take a peek inside their cars. You barely need the gift.

The day they finally killed Sadat, I was let go by Wendy's and I realized the world was playing hardball with me then. No more this woman will never have three nickels, or this guy gives in to cholesterol at age forty-eight in a laundromat, no: now I was reading page one news, and I couldn't stop.

I tried. I took a job at a carnival in Winston-Salem. There I was Madame Razora, Palmreader, and I could read the palms. The job paid very well, though it was only for ten days. The secret to palm reading, if you want to know, is don't look at the palm. Touch it with your fingertip, but while you do it look into the center of the person's eyes. Most of my customers in Winston-Salem are going to outlive me, do better with marriage, and go gray slower, so it wasn't too depressing. I was surprised to find two women who were going to marry the same man, but I figured they had something, so I never told them.

But the headlines kept showing for me at night in the trailer I rented. I saw the helicopters burning in the desert, which scared the shit out of me, because I didn't know what the hell that was and I thought I was finally just having nightmares. And I saw that plane hit the bridge in Washington D.C.

However, based on something I'd said to a young couple in Winston-Salem about their getting pregnant and having a job change, a man came to see me, the girl's father, Mr. Edwardo Shepherd, editor in chief of *The Realms of Twilight Tabloid News of the World*. He was a handsome gray-haired man of about fifty, and he said he wanted a "clairvoyant" for the paper's annual predictions and zodiac column. Clairvoyant. I laughed at the word. Clear seeing. If it was just that, oh God. But the pay was right and so I went to work.

I told them about Reagan and the election; I told them about the Russian spaceship breaking apart and where it would hit. He told me easy, lady. Nothing too hard. Those were his words, *too hard*, and they hit the nail on the head if anything does. He said, "Tell us something about Farrah Fawcett; tell us something about Reverend Moon." And he started coming to my apartment, this was in Tallahassee where the paper was located, and I saw that he was married, anybody can see that much about any man, but I was shot through with headlines and I needed some comfort. Can I say that?

I told him about John Lennon, maybe you remember our paper being investigated afterward, but I got a raise. Madame Zelena, Mistress of Doom. That was my byline. As I said, the Zelena part was all his, but "Mistress of Doom," that's in the target area all right. I was the Mistress of Doom for almost three years and—like I said—I hit ninety percent or so, missing on all the celebrity stuff right down the line.

Then Edwardo wanted something big. Circulation was down. They'd moved us out of the counter racks in Seven-Eleven to the newsstand, and advertising pages were off twenty percent. Edwardo was upset because of all that and because he was having to discount even the full-page ads now, ads like LISTEN TO BROTHER RUDY which ran every issue, a full page of small print mainly about how BROTHER RUDY could make a Mason jar full of money appear on your kitchen table. So Edwardo wanted something big. He told me he wanted something about World War III, something with H-Bomb in the headline, something with "millions will die, millions will be hideously deformed."

We met in a cafe on Crystal Avenue, an Italian dive called Ferdinand and Isabella's, and he told me he wanted something about Nuclear Holocaust. I smiled at him and told him Lady Di was going to have twin girls. He said again: "Something about THE BOMB, come on." I said, "No deal." He said, "Give me something with a mushroom cloud in it or take a walk." I looked at him. Men can be ugly sometimes. I told him an airliner was going to take out this entire block before dessert. He stood, as I knew he would. He said, "You can see the future and you won't tell me. You're fired, Madame Zelena, good-bye." I said to him, "You're right. I can sometimes see the future, like now I can see your wife is going to come to know that you have a lover."

And though I held no particular rancor for Edwardo, in fact no *particular* feeling at all, when he left I called his wife. Just because you're psychic, just because you can see the future, doesn't mean you can't make a little of it too.

And that, except for my first real enjoyable train trip and an incident in Albuquerque where I stopped and told a little Mexican boy that his dog was asleep three blocks away in an alley, brings me here, to the brink of the future. Isn't this a moment?

These are our lives, essentially carrying us forward, but we're only facing that way about half the time. All of us in this room except two couples and three girls (who are fairly certain), know where we'll be tomorrow night. Who we'll be with. What will be said. Many of us know what will not be said. But what is the past? I mean: I'd really like to know. Right now, tonight, my past seems to swirl before me like something I haven't really had yet. Like I said, it's the past that's the mystery; the future is here too, but just a simple series of pleasurable chores.

I can still see things in the same way as always. Somebody here has lost his wallet; I can see that. Should I tell him not to worry, that it fell out of his gray suit pants and is inside one of his fishing boots on the closet floor? No, that's not for me to say.

I've become—in these twelve years—an increasingly private person, whatever that means, and I face the future almost calmly. What do I see for me? A couple of good things. Some real good meals.

I will die because of a swimming incident off the coast of La Paz, Mexico. Brushed by a gray whale, I will lose the skin from my left thigh and buttock. The whale will touch me in play. Two days later I will die from an unchecked staphylococcus infection in the La Plage Hotel, room 37, which opens on a veranda. The largest organism and the smallest will do me in.

I will be in La Paz with a man who is in the audience tonight, a married man I haven't yet met. I can feel that he loves me a little right now. I don't blame him.

We will be on an illicit honeymoon, that's what he'll call it.

And how do I feel about the future? How do you feel? How do I feel about my death?—seeing it? I'm looking forward to the trip. I've never been to Mexico.

It will be wonderful to see that whale again.

# THE TIME
# I DIED

*I READ* a lot. I mean: I read *everything*. I always have. It used to really drive Grant crazy. My whole side of the bedroom was a hazard: stacks of pamphlets, magazines, papers, paperbacks, and about four dozen hardback books which I received from my book club and the library. But I love to read. Grant would say, "What's in that damn book, anyway?" But he really didn't want to know. I know this because several times I answered him. "Honey, this book is about Bud Sackett trying to deliver cattle to Santa Fe . . ." or "The woman in this article says she lost forty pounds of ugly fat by chewing each bite thirty-one times. . . ." But before I could finish the explanation, Grant was in the other room cranking the channels like he was trying to start an outboard motor.

I read a lot of trash. I do. I read *The Realms of Twilight Tabloid News of the World* from cover to cover. I've read all the stories about people coming back from the dead, and all twenty-one people have said about the same thing: there's that white room and some floating and their relatives and most of the time some music. I have also read some fine books, such as *Madame Bovary*, the biography of Dorothy Kilgallen called *Kilgallen*, which my book club sent me, and a large book called *The Gulag Archipelago*, a book which scared the devil out of Grant. "What language are you reading now?" he said.

Maybe I read too much. But I always felt it was better than drinking too much or chasing around. Later, that is what Grant got into. I suspected he was having troubles, and then I found out when he gave me herpes two. It's a virus. He stopped coming home. I really started reading.

I was reading fourteen hours a day. In one day I read *Are You a Genius? Great American Mystery Stories* (the whole volume), *The Book of Lists II*, and *Frankenstein*, which turned out to be different than I had ever thought. I was during this heavy reading period that Susan, my maid of honor, my best friend from high school, since before high school, called, and that led to how I died and why I'm in the hospital now.

Susan has a great attitude. She got married in high school to Andrew Botts, one of the most popular guys in our class, and then about three years ago, Andrew split. He's in California now, but Susan never let it get her down. She smiles about him like she knew it all along.

She used to call me up and talk, and then sometimes I'd have her over for dinner with Grant and me. Grant didn't like her, because he couldn't figure her out; but it was okay, because he would eat and then go in the other room and crank the channels, and Susan and I would talk for three hours. In fact, I'd rather be with Susan, talking, than alone reading in bed. She's a crazy woman and always has a new story about some new man in her life and what he's trying to get her to do now. She can laugh way down in her throat for about a minute without taking a breath.

So, when she called the last time she said she had heard about Grant leaving, and she laughed and said, "That's the real facts of life, Linda," which was exactly what she said at my wedding.

Anyway, she said I was definitely going to stop reading for one night and go out for a night with the girls. I had been reading back through a stack of *The Realms of Twilight Tabloid News of the World* at the time, and didn't want to go, because I was reading a pretty good series on UFO's, which have already picked up fifty-four people who have never been seen since and who are living better lives somewhere, according to their relatives and sometimes according to the sheriff. I was also rereading about the twenty-one people who had died and come back. Their stories all matched perfectly even though some of their stories were in different issues. It is their stories which really bother me, because now I have died and I *know* that there are twenty-one people who have fooled and lied to *The Realms of Twilight Tabloid News of the World*. But, when Susan called, I decided to close the papers and go out. Sometimes Susan can be just the wild thing I need.

When she picked me up in her Pinto, she told me we were going to a Daycare Fund Raiser at the Redwood Club, and that there would be a male stripper, and she laughed and blew cigarette smoke all over the windshield. I have read about male strippers in at least five magazines. The women all had good things to say in the articles, and in the pictures, the women looked like they were having a good time.

It was twelve dollars at the door, and the woman stamped our hands with a little purple star. The Redwood Club is just a big barroom with a real low sparkling ceiling. Susan knew a lot of the women there and we joined a table with three of her friends near the front. We had been drinking a little vodka in the car, and we had some more, and it was just flat fun being half high out of the house with a room full of women who were just roaring and carrying on.

There were actually two strippers. The first guy was announced as Rick. He came out to a record, the Supremes singing something, and he was very serious about removing his brown silk shirt, and then his brown silk pajama bottoms or whatever they were, and then he played a coy game of thumbs with his G-string for the rest of the song. The second and final song for Rick was The Four Seasons singing "Big Girls Don't Cry." He came stepping between the tables like a stretching cat, and Susan actually reached out and stuffed a dollar bill inside his jock along with all the other dollars hanging there like a bouquet.

I'm a buns person. Why that is, I don't know. But buns can start me up. I loved the arch of Rick's rear, and when he finally stripped off the G-string and flopped his petunia before us all, Susan and the girls went wild! Susan was laughing and bouncing in her seat and reaching for what she was calling "that banana." But Rick was a professional; I could tell by the way he kept just beyond an arm's length.

Then there was a very funny vodka intermission with everyone groaning and laughing and snorting and Susan laughing and asking me wasn't I glad I came, and you know, I was glad. Not because of Rick's buns, but because of a warm feeling I had. I really liked Susan and her attitude and the fact that she was a friend of mine.

In high school, when we were juniors, she stopped me after homeroom one morning in the spring and took my arm tightly and walked me down to her locker, smiling so her eyes nearly shut, and she told me she was going to get married. "You're the first person I've told," she said to me. "And you're the only person. Do me a favor," she laughed, "break it to our dear classmates." And then she said, "You know why we're doing it?" And she laughed so hard she dropped a book and could hardly get through her own answer, which she had to whisper: "To give the baby a father!" Then she straightened herself out and lifted her chin like a queen and walked off down the corridor, turning once to announce: "The facts of life."

Now, I'm no good judge of penises. Grant had one, I'm sure.

He must have, I think. But the next stripper, Doug, made it clear from his entrance on, that he was out to set new standards for us all. Susan was crazy for him. He would back way up then open his shirt and stride toward the audience as if he was going to jab us all with that heavy G-string. Everyone would scream when he did that. Susan couldn't stop laughing. She did yell: "What have you got in there anyway, Dougie?" And everybody thought the same thing: that is not all him. Susan would yell, "What is that, a shoe?" and the Redwood Club would just go nuts. But at the end of the third song (Doug stretched his strip to three records), which was Elvis singing "My Way," we all found out the truth. He turned his back on us and flexed his buns in a way that almost made me shudder, and he flipped his G-string into the fourth row, another eruption of screaming, and he rotated to us revealing the most god-awful THING—and that is the right word, "THING"—in the whole world. It looked like a hammer. The place exploded. There was more screaming than if there'd been a fire. He lobbed it around for a good while, and I'm sure people passing by in cars could hear The Redwood Club rising off the earth. It's lucky for me I like buns, I told Susan, or I would have embarrassed myself. A lot of women did.

After that session died down, we plunged outside and the fresh air really made us drunk. Susan hopped on the hood of her car and leaned against the windshield. The sky was full of stars. It was funny sitting there. I thought: all these stars, are they out every night? I'd never seen the stars before. We sat on her car and drank a little more vodka. Susan had been sweating and the hair over her face was wet in a little fringe. She was smiling, kind of wicked, like she knew things were going to be like this all along. After a while, she said, "You know, all this entertainment has made me kind of hungry. Let's go eat."

We went over to Rose's, where I'd never been at night before, and the place was empty except for Leo, Rose's husband, who served us two Burrito Specials and cold beer. God, it was fun sitting there at night, like being girls. When Leo would bring another beer, Susan would keep her head down, her eyes under her eyebrows going to his crotch, and then back to my eyes, and we'd laugh until we couldn't even eat. It was like we had this great big secret on all men.

Grant had never liked to go out to dinner with me. I always liked to read the whole menu, every word. For me it's part of the pleasure of dining out. Grant liked to order the same thing all the time: spaghetti or burgers. He'd order and I wouldn't be through reading Column A. I loved to read phrases in some of the places like "nestled amid french fries aplenty" or even "smothered with onions." I always ordered the item which was the most well written. I don't need to tell you what Grant thought of that.

The rest of the night with Susan happened a little too quickly. We were driving down Front Street and we hit the hill a bit fast, and Susan couldn't make the corner. That part went slow. We drifted wide in the turn, and when the tire hit the island between the four lanes, I looked at Susan, and she was still smiling like this was all expected. The Pinto wouldn't straighten up. It rose over the island and gently and quietly steered into the deserted lobby of the Cambert Hotel. Grant and I spent our wedding night at the Cambert Hotel, and as the glass doors burst and I saw the front desk, I knew I was going to die. There was no sound. The last thing I felt was my back coming through my chest, and I was dead.

Now, this is the real part: it was not a white room. I did not float above a white room. There was no white room into which my relatives floated one at a time. Do you see? There was no white room. It was not a room at all, but a tiny cave, black as black, no light whatsoever. No relatives drifting in to hug me.

I felt like I'd been hammered in the little cave, and there was a pair of sunglasses underneath my right hip, poking me. It really hurt. I could feel the cave wall with my hands and the wall was damp and cold, and I could tell I was stuck. There were piles and piles of old shoes on top of me and *there was no music.* I listened for a long time and there was a little noise, it was a distant rasping, muffled by all the shoes, and it sounded like a fork on a pie plate. Then it was quiet for I don't know how long. I couldn't move and I couldn't go to sleep. But there was no music. I waited and waited, just feeling those sunglasses under my thigh, and I thought any minute I might hear Susan laughing or see some person in a white robe coming to greet me. Nothing. I was smothering under all those shoes in a dark cave, rubbing my fingertips up and down the walls feeling the slime, and I did this for a long time. I mean, up to what I thought was three or four weeks. Nothing. And I came to know that this was it: I was dead, that's all. I wished I had something to read. But even if I'd had something, it was too dark. I did get kind of mad at those twenty-one liars who had made money spinning fibs to *The Realms of Twilight Tabloid News of the World.*

Later I heard some quiet chipping noises, like someone putting cups away. Then in the quiet dark, I realized that I was going to come back from the dead. All that happened was this: the rock became softer and I stretched my legs through it and pushed my hands through it and reached around and removed that damn pair of sunglasses jabbing my butt and the shoes floated away and I leaned my head back into the soft putty-like rock and I was in this bed. A moment later Dr. Fergus came in and used his little flashlight on me.

Later still, Grant came by and brought me some magazines and said some words while I lay very still and squinted at his crotch.

So, all I want to say is this. I've read those god-damned liars in the papers, and I'm here to tell you there's no white room. I crashed into the lobby of the Cambert Hotel, where I spent my wedding night, and I was killed along with my best friend since before high school, Susan McArgul. And after being dead for three and half weeks my time, and almost four minutes your time, I was allowed to return from being dead. Susan McArgul didn't get to return. Now, those are the real facts of life.

# THE USES
# OF VIDEOTAPE

*EVERYTHING* that happens when I sleep does not need explanation, only some things. I am sixty-six years of age, which seems about right. Lorraine is sixty-six years of age as well, and this, if you think about it, is simply a coincidence. We have both been married forty-one years, because we are married to each other. And now, in the nights when the bedspread leaves for the floor, after such an epoch of remaining on the bed, I want to know why.

The bedspread is the center of my inquiry and is becoming the main topic in my conversations. Lorraine, who has made the bed every day for forty-one years, is not interested. She is not the one who wakes up cold in the morning; she is not the one of us who anticipates being cold when we lie for sleep.

Before I leave in the morning, I come back in and point at it and tell her: "The bedspread." She is under the covers and it cannot matter. When I come home from the hospital at night, the spread is back in place waiting to trick me again.

So it is the main topic in my conversations. Oh, not with the other janitors, I do not mention this affliction to them. I talk to Jerome, the son, the offspring of our hearts. He is married, but does not live in the city. At their house, Lilly fixes the coffee and Jerome tells me to forget it, to purchase an electric blanket if I am cold. That I become chilled is not the point. Lilly tells me not to worry about it, and Lorraine concurs by saying nothing, but asks instead about seven topics which they have going by and by. I have stood up at their own table, interrupting everything, to indicate that I do worry and I should worry about these occurrences in my household which have begun at so late a date.

This is not a way to act and I know it, and when I have apologized, Jerome asks then if I have any theories, if perhaps I should pin the bedspread to the blanket. I will not stoop to pins, and I am shouting. I love Lilly as my own. She is so dear I tremble for her happiness, and I am blessed to have my own son, Jerome, married to such loveliness. It is a heartache that she thinks that I am no longer a sensible man.

Then, every week when we visit them, I shut up, but it leaves me unable to think. I stare at the table and Lilly's flowers and see only the spread knotted on the floor. My staring bothers Lilly, and my heartache is multiplied. Lorraine is not worried. She knows me, and she drinks her coffee. There have been worse items in a marriage. Luckily, it is not affecting my work.

From time to time, when I talk to only Jerome about it, he is logical, and I appreciate that, but it does not help. I took his advice once and stayed up until after three in the morning, sitting in a chair watching the bedspread, but it did not move, and I wore the next day across my back like a fire. I cannot ask Lorraine, my wife, to sit up for me. That she is steady is at least a minor comfort in this tribulation. Then Jerome begins to get the look on his face for me too, and he has new and final advice.

### T W O

*I TOLD* the man I am sixty-six years old and feel odd renting this machine. He rewound the reels and then ran the pictures of ourselves in the showroom. He pointed to the man next to him in the television and told me that it was me. The picture was all gray, but they were my clothes.

That night, when Lorraine is asleep, I am up again, assembling the cords and the components. The components fit easily, like the man said, and I am like a boy on the carpet, plugging everything with three prongs together and everything with two prongs together. Erected, the camera does not look like something that belongs in my house, but it will do for one night. Because I have only four hours of video tape, I must sit until two in a chair with one lamp and the hospital newsletter. When it is after two and the camera sees it all, I climb into the bed wondering if I can sleep now with the small lamplight.

Lorraine cannot sense my exhilaration in the morning when I wake and the spread is gone away again, and the camera is still turning. I have recorded it all. "Do not touch this rented equipment," I tell her. "I will be home this evening and talk to you."

This is a wonderful day with a purpose. It is a very clean hospital, and the staff receives notice of their good work from Dr. Richter. He speaks to me personally, and his questions show his respect for me, which I return. And the drive home is like a long breath. I am free, going home to see at last the solution to the problem. There is simplicity in the way all the cars go in their ways.

At home, I start with Lorraine, but she is not interested in the equipment and what I have done. She goes after a while to the telephone to talk to her friends of other topics. After rewinding the equipment, I sit in the chair in the bedroom and begin witnessing the videotape. Though I can stop it with a switch, I ask Lorraine to bring my dinner in, because the show is almost four hours in length.

The light is gray, like in the showroom, and I see myself go in bed. Though I do not look like that, I trust the machine. The spread is over the man and the wife; the man is on the near side. I know his thoughts, and I think I can see the instant sleep arrives for him. I watch the two people sleeping while I eat my dinner. Lorraine looks for a minute, but moves elsewhere in the house. She is moving in the way she does before she goes in bed.

The tape seems endless, reel to reel, and I watch the grayness of sleep. Lorraine comes to bed and turns off her lamp. She is a kind woman, and I have known her for a long time in this life. Her form under the covers is the continuity of my days. On the screen the gray light does not change; the equipment hums like sleep.

Lorraine is breathing up the night, and I sit in my chair until the gray light goes white and then the tape slaps and flickers, so I turn off the equipment. I have watched the entire program, and I trust the machine. Near the end I could see the bedspread on the floor. After a while the man arose in his pajamas, and I could see his feet standing by the rumpled spread. I watched the entire videotape, and I did not see it move. It was on the man; then it was on the floor.

I dismantle the components and coil the cords, and I climb onto the bed with my wife Lorraine. We were born in the same year. I pull the covers to my ears, feeling the quilted bedspread in my fingers. I put my hand on Lorraine's side, and she turns halfway to me, not asleep at all. "You thought it was me." She laughs, moving the bed. She laughs with enjoyment. "You thought," the bed is moving, "that it was me." This requires that I too laugh, and she moves to me fully now, laughing in our bed. The bedspread will work its little magic every night, a new thing I must accept within this life.

# PHENOMENA

*FIRST* of all, I'm not one of these people who ever wanted to see a UFO, an unidentified flying object. I have never wanted to see an unidentified anything. The things in my life, I identify; that's good with me. I'm not one of these people who is strange or weirded-out over unexplainable phenomena. I don't want any phenomena at all, and we're lucky in Cooper, because there isn't much phenomena. About the time there is a little phenomena, I identify the phenomena and throw them in jail.

I'm the sheriff.

So I'm not a weirdo. Things happen sometimes and I do my best. My name is Derec Ferris, and I've traced the Ferrises back all the way to Journey City, near the border, and there isn't a weirdo in the whole bunch. Now, I'm the sheriff; you notice I didn't say I'm the law around here. Whitney used to say he was the law around here. That was when he was sheriff. I can tell you exactly when he stopped saying that. Four years ago in September. We were together in his car late one night after coffee at The World, and we nailed this speeder right down from the high school. A rented Firebird, gunmetal gray. Actually we flashed him on the curve of Quibbel's Junk Yard and it took us the whole mile of town to slow down.

We pulled him over in front of Cooper Regional, where Whitney and I had been Cougars for four years together. It was about two in the morning. Whitney put his hand on my arm and went up to the Pontiac. I could see he was working up his sarcastic rage; he used to say that eighty percent of being a good sheriff was acting. Anyway, he starts: "Who do you think you are, endangering the lives of the citizens of Cooper by whipping through here at eighty-two miles an hour?" And the guy goes: "I'm Dan Blum, and I'm late. Who do you think you are?" Whitney loves that, an opening. "I'm Whitney Shields and I'm the law around here." Well, Dan Blum, as his name actually turned out to be, thought that was the funniest thing he'd ever heard, and after a little chuckle, he said, "Say, that's great. So, it's your wife that sleeps with the law." That comment seemed to confuse Whitney, even though he slapped the guy for seventy-five big ones, and he never said that about being the law again.

That was, like I said, four years ago, and since then Whitney's in-laws have had troubles outside Chicago, and he and Dorothy, who was also a Cougar with us, and whom I had also known for forty-one years, moved over there, and they might as well be on another world for all I hear from them. This is all to say, I'm not the law. I'm fifty-five years old and I've lived in this county all my life, except for fourteen months when I lived in Korea employed by Uncle Sam. My name is Derec Ferris and that's who sleeps with my wife.

The fact is, I'm still surprised that Whitney left. I mean, where is he? I still expect to see him squashing his stool at the counter at The World every time I walk in there. Hell, he grew up here along the river just like I did; he and I and Harold were the three musketeers. We worked for Nemo at Earth Adventure two summers in high school, and we gained four hundred and forty-four yards passing as Cooper Cougars in 1949, setting a record that stood until 1957. Then: poof! he's gone, and I'm sheriff. I've got his car and everything. It still smells like him.

I don't want to talk about it. At all. What I want to talk about is the Unidentified Object that has come into my life, the whole unidentified flying object day, so that you can see I'm not a phenomena weirdo; I'm only Derec Ferris, the sheriff here in Cooper.

First of all, I'm not going to give you any theory, because I don't have any. And I don't want any. Where did it come from? I don't care. I've been here in Cooper all my life and it might have come from over in Mercy or even Griggs. It kind of looked like something from Griggs. I don't care. It was a UFO. It might have come from Korea; try to tell me that's on this earth. And why did it come? *Please.* I'm going to give you the day, the whole day, and—really—nothing but the day.

First thing: Sarah calls. She says we received a card from Derec; that's our son, same name. He works for a textbook publisher in Palo Alto, California, and he's a painter. Paints pictures. Well, it's a little news, because we haven't seen him in five years, and we don't get that much mail. Every time I drive by Cooper Regional I think about him, though. Even then when he was in high school refusing to play football, he said he couldn't wait to get out of here, Cooper, and go to California. Which he did. I feel bad about it, and I miss him, but I figure it this way: at least somebody got what he wanted.

Sarah says that Derec is going to have a show. Well. I don't know what that is, and she explains that it is a show of his paintings and it is good news. She wants to go. She is excited on the telephone. I tell her great, but there's a radio call coming in, I'll talk to her later, and I hang up. I thought: I want to go, too.

I want to go and hold down my stool at The World and drink my gallon of coffee, but Arvella the dispatcher says it's something from Nemo out at Earth Adventure, a bear attack or something. So I lock up and I drive out to Earth Adventure.

On the way out I'm thinking about Derec and his show, and I'm kind of blue thinking about what he ever thinks of his old man. Did you ever do that, wonder what your grown kids think of you? The times you tried, the times you didn't try. No matter who you are, I think, you still want your boy to be like you. Derec *is* like me, with his ears, and he's got the build, but the rest . . . I don't know.

Old Earth Adventure is about on its last legs. If you didn't know where you were going, I doubt you could find the place. The two terrific signs Nemo put up before Harold, Whitney, and I worked for him are all peeled to hell, and a Chinese elm has taken the best one, the one with the dinosaur peeking over at the boatload of people. You can still see the profile of the dinosaur poking up above the sign, but you can't read a word through the bushes.

It turned out not to be a bear attack. I knew it wouldn't be. Nemo's bear, Alex, hasn't been awake for about two years. It turned out to be Monty, the old cougar, who must be forty now and who's lost most of his hair and teeth and whose skin sags off his bones like it was somebody else's suit; Monty had fallen out of a tree and broke his hind leg on the hood of some tourist's Ford. By the time I arrived, Monty had already dragged himself into the women's restroom and he was growling in the corner like an old man getting ready for his last spit. His poor old rheumy eyes were full of tears. Hell, I'd known him from a kitten when they found him west of Mercy at the Ringenburgs', crying in the barn being harassed by a dozen swallows. I'd fed that cat a lot of corndogs the summer I was seventeen and worked the boats.

So I kept guard by the women's room door, so nobody would

get a surprise, while we waited for Doctor Werner to come out from town. The guy from the Ford was arguing, or trying to argue, with Nemo about the damage and the scare and the hazard, and all Nemo would do was point at me and say, "There's the sheriff." But the guy wasn't coming near me or the shack where Monty was dying. Finally he left and the vet pulled up in his black van. I stayed with him while he drugged the big old cat. Then Werner and Nemo had a little talk outside while I watched Monty's tongue loll farther and farther out of his mouth. Just above him in the stall, somebody had carved "Kill All Men" in uneven printing.

When the two men came back they had decided that this was it for Monty, and Werner said he'd haul him off. But Nemo said no, said to put him to sleep right there in the women's room, so Werner did. Monty, who was already asleep, didn't even quiver.

Then Nemo and Werner argued about money for a while, Nemo trying to give the doc a twenty and the doctor not even looking Nemo in the face, saying, "No way, Nemo, not this time. No charge." They pushed that twenty back and forth twenty times like two men in a restaurant, and finally the vet climbed in his van and headed out.

Nemo stood there with his twenty still in his hand in the middle of the dirt road and said he was pretty close to it this time. If he lost any more animals, Earth Adventure would have to close. You couldn't charge people four bucks a car to drive along a half mile dirt road to see one bear sleeping in a way that showed his worn out old ass, a plastic tiger Nemo had gotten from the Exxon station in Clinton, six peacocks, and four hundred geese. "It was different with a mountain lion," he said. "Monty was *something*."

Old Nemo. I told him not to worry, he still had the underground canal trips, but that wasn't too good either, since the boats—the same boats I worked—are in pretty bad condition. One sank last summer out from under a family from Mercy. It was lucky for Nemo the boat went down just outside the tunnel, where the water is only a foot deep, or he'd have had genuine legal action.

So I stood there with old Nemo, looking around at Earth Adventure crumbling in the weeds. I could see it clearly: the closed sign across his gate next summer. After a while, he thumbed his overall strap and went to get an old canvas mail bag and started filling it with the round white rocks that he uses to line the paths.

"Can I help you, Nemo?" I said, and he opened the bag.

"Right here," is all he said.

So I lifted Monty, who must have weighed ninety pounds, and Nemo helped guide him into the bag. He cinched the tie and started dragging the bag toward the canal. When we got there, he wanted to put it in one of the boats, and by the time I'd helped him do that, I was committed. He climbed in the bow of the old peeling boat and there was that seat in the stern. I found one paddle in the weeds and took my place. The boat was so weathered and shot I couldn't tell which one it had been; it could have been mine once.

When I was seventeen, we came out here—Whitney, Harold, and I—and Nemo hired us piecework. We each had a boat and we got seventy-five cents a tour. In those days Nemo had a little dock strung with Christmas lights, and summer nights it was great. There was a popcorn stand right there too, so people could feed the ducks, all those mallards tame as barnducks in the bright water. We'd tear the tickets and Whitney would feed them to the ducks whenever he ran out of other bad jokes.

I'd get five people in my boat, and I'd pole off. "These are the natural wonders of Cooper," I'd say as we entered the cave. "They were formed a million million years ago. They have found albino perch in these waters and there may still be creatures as yet undiscovered beneath us. The legend is that a trip through this wonder makes you five years younger or five years older depending on how you've treated your mother and father. Please keep your hands inside the boat."

Now Nemo perched on his seat, his knees together, as I steered us out into the cool dark of the cavern. I hadn't been in here for years. I used to have to come down and chase teenagers out and break up their beer parties, but it wasn't too hard, because I knew my way around. There in the quiet dark with Nemo, I could almost hear Harold doing his romantic version of the tour for his boat. It was like singing. Or Whitney kidding with the passengers, laughing and telling off-color jokes, "Keep your hands inside the boat, not there, buddy. Lady, keep your hands to yourself; just because it is dark there is no need to turn into an aborigine." The passengers in his boats would laugh and call back and ahead and go "Wooo-woooo!" And at the other end, Whitney always got the tips.

For me it was a job. I was saving for a car that turned out to be a used 1939 Buick. For Harold, it was romantic, each little trip got him a little. He believed it; he even painted a name on his boat: The Santa Maria. For Whitney, it was fun.

And then later, after I met Sarah, we all used to stay around almost every night, make a tour or two. Stop in the middle, bump around in the boats. It smelled nice then, like sand and willows, before the water treatment plant went in and raised the temperature. The five of us would take a boat in. Whitney and a date, Sarah and I, and Harold. Whitney would start on his spiel about how no virgin had ever emerged from these caverns, and he would let Sarah and me off midway on the limestone ledge, and then he'd take Harold to the far end where Harold would sit with his guitar and just play and play. Sometimes he'd sing, "Stormy Weather" or "Pennies From Heaven." Sarah and I would eat the popcorn and talk about high school or the families who came to Earth Adventure. We could hear Whitney hauling around in the boat, saying, "Come on; come on," to some girl from Mercy, a waitress, or somebody he'd picked up that night. He and I were clearly different that way. I never touched a girl casually in my life, not to this day. Whitney never touched them any other way. And I guess, Harold never touched one at all. I don't know. Anyway, they were great nights.

When Nemo and I passed the ledge, he lifted his hand and looked ahead. There was one rock column and then we could see the end, the rough triangle of light that opened on the river.

"This is good right here," he said.

He started to stand, but I motioned him down, and I got up and took hold of the bag. I set it carefully on the gunwale and looked at Nemo. All I could see against the light was his silhouette, and it didn't move. I waited. He didn't say anything, so I set the bag out and let the water take it.

*NOW,* remember, this is the day of the phenomenon. I went back to the jail and filed the report and by then it was lunchtime. I went over to The World and had the liver and onions for an hour. All that reminiscing had me hungry.

It was Monday, like I said, and so I knew they'd have a workout at the high school. I parked across the tennis court with the radio on in case Arvella came up with something, and watched practice. Well, here it was only the second week of school, still summer really, so I knew no one would be breaking his back, but still, I was disappointed when one of the coaches blew the whistle and the practice fell apart and the kids sauntered off toward the gym. I had been dreaming a little, but I still didn't see anything that was going to beat Griggs. For a minute I thought of the sheriff going over to the two coaches and giving them a word to the wise. But: nope.

It made me a little sad, sitting there in the car after the field had emptied. Football. As great as it was for Whitney and me, football was one of the first things Derec and I argued about. I couldn't understand why he didn't want to play, but after I saw that he really didn't want to, I let it go. I didn't care if he played or didn't; it wasn't worth fighting over. But I don't think he ever understood that. I think to the day he left Cooper he thought I was disappointed. As a man, sometimes, I find there are some things I can do nothing about. The words just won't line up in my mouth.

I went down to The World for my evening coffee until it was dark and then I got the call from Arvella, the only other call that day. Somebody was injured out to the Passion Play Center. I have a call or two out there every summer. Somebody gets a snakebite behind the stage or a flat settles on somebody's foot as they're shifting scenery in the dark. But this time I was a little worried because Arvella said, as she was signing off, that she thought it was Harold Kissel. And Harold is now pushing three hundred pounds and if he missed a step out of his trailer or fell off the apron, it would be serious.

I've been told that every community has a Harold Kissel, my old friend. I doubt it. He'd moved to Cooper with his mother when we were in tenth grade and for two years everybody thought he was from New York, and he didn't tip his hand about it either. His manners were amazing. I mean it was amazing that he had any, because I guess, none of the rest of us did. But he had a hat, a dark derby sort of hat and he'd tip it, and he'd hold doors for about everybody, and the things he'd do with his napkin even in The World were worth watching. It's funny, but he never took much guff for any of it, everybody just kind of knew him: eccentric. That's why I liked him and why he was the only friend I had who wasn't on the football team.

He wasn't allowed to go to Korea either, which was a relief for just about everybody in town, because by that time, the year after we graduated, everybody liked Harold in their own way. While I was gone, he started and became director of the Cooper Players and was just known for that. He was the theater. Sarah wrote me about the productions. She helped sew costumes, even the curtain for the stage at the old Episcopal Church.

When I came back from Korea, which is a cold place mostly, Sarah and I were married in the Lutheran Church, and Harold was one of the ushers along with Whitney who was also best man. The first year I was a deputy, Harold's mother died, and he went away. Sarah was real worried. She and Whitney's wife, Dorothy, had been in two plays by then. They kind of starred in *Arsenic and Old Lace* as the aunts. You should have seen Sarah as an old lady. I told her right then that I'd love her my whole life, because even with white hair and big gray lines all over her face, she was too pretty to stand. Oh, and they were also in *Julius Caesar* after that. They were two Roman soldiers, which was pretty goofy in my opinion, but it was okay, because about nine people total saw that deal. So when Harold's mother passed away, Sarah was worried. There was a lot of talk. The Playhouse, as they were calling the church, had added a lot to Cooper, especially in the winter, and people said it would be a shame to lose it.

Where he went for four years, nobody knows. I know that, because he never told me. Some say he finally went to New York and there was a rumor about his going to France or Africa. No clues. When he came back, he had the beginnings of the fat and

he looked worn. Hell, we all do. He had a meeting of the old
Cooper Players and announced that what this town needed was
"a passion play."

That was thirty years ago. The passion play has become the
biggest thing about Cooper really. People say, "Have you been
over to the Cooper Passion Play?" It's a real institution. Every
summer thousands of people see Harold play the life of Christ,
and I've seen it quite a few times myself. The local joke is that
whenever anybody says Jesus H. Christ, the H. stands for Harold.

He's real good in all the parts where he's among the children
and disciples. He knows how to walk and he's got great hand
movements, but the part which everyone remembers, the part
which has been told across the counter in The World ten thousand
times is when the music starts and the lights go out. The last
thing you see is Mary Magdalene and the others on their knees
weeping and praying and then the darkness in the amphitheater,
just the sky with all our stars, sometimes the moon on a little
cloud cruise, and the music real low and sad along with the sound
effects of some hammering.

Then, Harold climbs those stairs behind the cross and steps
out and places his arms on the crossbars, his head hung down at
the perfect angle, and pow! the spotlight puts everybody's eyes
out with the white circle of Jesus on the cross: you can feel the
chilly waves of goose bumps cross over the whole audience. Even
his bald spot jumps at you in the scene like a halo. I remember
listening to his voice in the Earth Adventure Caverns as he sang,
"Stormy Weather," and I know he's just a man with the God-
given ability to give others the chills.

The cross had come down while Harold was setting his arms
up on the crossbar. The cross was old and Harold was heavy. The
old timber leaned over and ripped out of the stage like a tree in
a storm. They said it sounded like a bomb. Harold had hit the

stage hard and there was blood and make-up blood everywhere. He wasn't moving. The cross had clobbered Bonnie Belcher who was playing Mary Magdalene and a high school girl from Mercy, but they were both okay, just lots of blood. They hadn't moved a thing. Feely told me they were afraid they would break his back. So, I had it all right there. I thought this is what happens: Whitney is gone, dead to me, and now Harold is killed.

I knelt over him, but I couldn't feel a pulse and I couldn't tell if he was breathing. In that loincloth he looked like a great big dead kid, a two-year-old. By this time I was crying, or tears were just coming, I don't know. And I didn't care. I had to get Feely and Jerry—who plays Judas—to help me lift the cross off Harold and we dragged it back and dropped it off the rear of the stage. Then I heard this noise. Clapping. Out there in the dark, about half the audience still waited to see what was going to happen to Jesus now. It must have looked pretty strange to see the sheriff bending over him. And it was strange for me too; I couldn't see the people at all.

I was scared. We wrestled Harold into the ambulance and he never made a noise, not a gurgle or a groan. Then Jerry shut the doors and Boyce drove away. Jerry turned to me and said, "You better say something, Derec. The people aren't leaving." There I was out there in the dark talking to Judas in his nightgown, Jerry Beemer, who is going to be the assistant manager at the Dairy Creme in Griggs all his goddamned life, and he is instructing me as to what I had better do. And what really made me boil, on top of being sick and scared, was that I knew he was right. I went back up onto the stage in the lights and stood in front of the blood stain and said, "He's going to be all right, folks. You can go home now. And be careful driving. Those of you parked to the side can slip back to 21 through Gilmers' place, even though it is the entrance."

It was real quiet for a second, but then I heard the shuffling, and the families sorted themselves out and went off in the dark.

ON the way home I didn't want to see another thing. I didn't want to see the UFO. I'd seen enough for one day already. I just wanted to see Sarah. It was after one in the morning and I just wanted to see her. She'd be asleep, which was good because I didn't want to go over anything again. I try not to tell her any of what goes on with my work; it's all either ridiculous or hideous—who wants to hear that? If she asks me about something, I try to wait and let it pass. I can wait.

There's a lot inside a man that never gets out; I don't understand that or pretend to understand it, but if women ever knew that those waits, those times that I stir my coffee, twenty times right, twenty times left, were just full, full of the way a day crams my heart full, if women knew how much was in a man, they'd never let up. But there's nothing I can do about it. The worse something is, the deeper I keep it. That's the law.

If Sarah won't let it go, if she gets on me, I have a simple strategy: I turn and ask when she's going to have that rummage sale and get rid of some of the junk in the garage and the basement. That'll start her. She's a woman who has saved everything she's ever had in her hand. I won't go into it, but she has a box of egg cartons once touched by her Uncle Elias and they remind her of him. Actually, they do me too.

Anyway, I don't tell her all the ugly details of being sheriff. And I especially didn't want to tell her about Harold and how he fell and killed himself. All I want to do is see her there sleeping and to crawl into the bed by her.

It was 1:20 A.M. I was driving home and I was a tired man. Now get ready. At 13 and 30, where I turn for home, there at Chernewski's Tip-a-Mug, I saw the UFO. It sat down in the road right in front of me. Actually, I heard it as I slowed for the four way. There was a clanking—awful—like a pocket knife in the drier. I mean a real painful sound, some machine about to die, and then: *whomp*! The whole contraption dropped onto Route 30, hard as a wet bale.

At first I thought a combine had turned over; I didn't know what was going on. I couldn't see it too well. It just sat there clanking and hissing. I could also hear it spitting oil on the pavement; honest to god, this UFO was a wreck. I stood out of the car. I could see all the terrible plumbing caging several gray oil drums and rusty boxes, and lots of little ladders, some missing rungs. The wiring ran along the outside of the heavy ductwork, taped there by somebody in a hurry.

Then the smell hit me. It had been burning oil and something else, something like rubber or plastic. The fumes were thick, billowing off one side just like the train wreck over at Mercy when the asphalt truck got creamed last winter.

I was going to go up to the thing to see if anybody was hurt, but the way it was settling, jumping around like a winged duck, and banging, I was afraid it would all give way and fall right on me.

Besides, about then I saw the alien. A door slammed open right then, falling out like the gate on the back of a pickup. And I stood there in the dark while the alien climbed down.

Now the alien, the alien. The alien looked a lot like my boy, Derec. To me, the alien looked like my son. It was a kid about twenty-three years old wearing a sleeveless white T-shirt with the words JOHN LENNON on the front. He wore greasy green surgical pants and tennis shoes. No socks. He jumped onto Route 30 and walked past me this close and looked in the backseat of the car. Then he folded his hands like this, across his chest like he was confused. Then he looked in again and put his hands on top of the car like this, like he was waiting to be frisked or just thinking it all over. I don't know what he'd expected to be in the car, but it wasn't there. Then I found out. He looked at me, and this is going to sound like a weirdo, like some airbrain who likes these encounters, but he looked in that moment just like Derec. He said to me, "Where's Harold?"

Well, I was a little surprised by that. I didn't know what to say. And I didn't have to say anything. He skipped past me again, walking just like Derec, bouncing a little in those tennis shoes, and he climbed back up in that crazy rig. He had to slam that tailgate hatch or whatever it was four times to get it to stay closed, and the last time I heard glass break and sprinkle onto Route 30.

I stepped back, watching all the time. The UFO cranked itself up into a frenzy, the hissing made me squint. He had it revved up and shaking, just a raw sound for three or four minutes, more than any engine I know could take. Then it jumped, and that's the right word: *jumped*, ten feet straight up, and it came down again hard, really shaking, and then it jumped and hovered up over Route 30. As it climbed up a little ways, I could see a small propeller on the under carriage—and the oil was dripping onto that and it sprayed me a good one going by. After I couldn't see the UFO anymore or hear it, thank God, or smell it, all I could hear were the crickets and the buzzing of Chernewski's Tip-a-Mug neon sign with that silly cocktail glass tipped and fizzing the three green bubbles, and all there was left on the road was the worst oil spill you'd want to see. I went over to it and it was oil all right, dirty oil that hadn't been changed in five or six thousand miles of hard driving, and I found all these pieces of glass. Looks like some kind of Mason jar. And I found this one bolt. It's left-handed. The oil stain is still out there—over both lanes, for you to see for yourselves. You can't miss it: four or five gallons—at least.

That was the UFO.

*I WAS* a boy in this town. And now I am a man in this town. A lot of things happen some days. Somebody'll die and there'll be a mattress in the backyard. Some kid driving a hard hangover and an asphalt truck won't see a train and there'll be smoke, clear to Griggs. And somedays nothing happens. The flies won't move five inches down the counter in The World. Some days things happen, and some days nothing does, but at the end of each I have to lie down. I lie by Sarah, the collector of treasures, in our bed which is surrounded by rooms full of the little things of our lives. She still has the ticket stubs from the game with Mercy, our first date, and they too sleep in some little box in some drawer in our house. I lie by Sarah in my place on earth, and slowly— it takes hours—I empty for the earth to turn and prepare me for the next thing, another day.

Sarah is in the bed under the covers in the shape I will always identify. Her form is identifiable. "The hospital called," she says. She's awake. I button my pajamas and don't answer. I don't want to get started. I don't want to get started on Harold and go over the whole thing. I climb heavily into bed. "Delores called from the hospital." I weigh nine hundred pounds; sleep is coming up around my eyes like warm water. "Delores called from the hospital. She said Harold is going to be all right."

I float in the bed by my wife Sarah's side. I know she is going to go on. "I made reservations for Palo Alto, for Derec's show.

We're going next Thursday, so get the time off. You want to go, don't you?"

"Yeah," I say. "Yeah." Sleep rises in me like sweet smoke. It is late here in Cooper. It kind of feels late everywhere. Maybe it is just late for me. My son Derec. We're going to Palo Alto, California. We're going to fly out there.

# III

# HALF LIFE

*APRIL FOOL'S* morning I spotted the salt and pepper shaker right away. They are never on the table, but suddenly at breakfast there they were, right in front of Paris's smiling face.

"Are you ready for school?" I asked.

"Yep, I've already eaten." She looked at my grapefruit.

Okay, I thought. I'll bite. I lifted the salt shaker and turned it slowly over the dish. Nothing. The lid stayed on. I shook it.

"April Fool!" Paris laughed.

Stacey turned from the counter. "She got you, eh?"

"Oh, and, Dad, I've changed schools. I'm going to Astronaut Training Institute." Paris made her face very grave. "Uintah is fine, but I've decided to be a . . ." She looked up at Stacey for the support that gave them both away. "Space Cadet!" I gave her the smile back and she was able to say, "April Fools!" happily.

"You and Jake Garn. Let's head out," I said, grabbing my coat, case, and keys from the sideboard.

"Michael," Stacey stopped me. "Remember to pick up Dalton today." She handed me one of her memo sheets with the flight number and time on it.

"Now say 'April Fool's,'" I said. Paris was already out in the pickup.

"Michael. Be nice. It's just three days. I'll be in court until after five. Just bring him back here and get settled in. I'll meet you at seven at the Park Cafe."

I grabbed her in both arms, dropping all my gear, pressing her fiercely back against the counter, covering her mouth with mine, trying to get a hand under her folded arms and onto a breast. Despite her fussing it was a great kiss and a sweet minor struggle.

"Oh the jury would love to see this," she said. "My credibility would soar."

"It's April," I said, kissing her quickly again. "Good luck in court. Keep your arms folded; it's very effective."

I didn't like Dalton. Six years ago he had been one of my students at Dorcet. A lot of my former students come to visit; they remember me as the person who taught them *Huck Finn* or *Gatsby*. Some remember the comments I scribbled on the bottom of their compositions. They are now writing for *Institutional Investor* or *Business Week*, and they have a week to ski and they come West to see us. I am their old teacher and they remember the way I scolded and fostered the children they were. And I like most of them. They remind me of things I said when I was young, and it makes me feel good to have once been wise, and I wonder how it escaped me, that wisdom. I just remember being a young teacher and trying hard.

But Dalton was one of those students I didn't care for. He took English the way others take two weeks in Jamaica: casually. He was rich and good-looking as a seventeen-year-old senior and he glided through school with an athlete's grace, studying nothing harder than the forward pass. I'm not saying he was dumb. No, he knew he would go from Dorcet to Yale, where his father was a trustee and where he would major in economics and from there drop into Manhattan for Goldman Sachs or Fenner DeWitt.

What I'm saying is he had that special kind of arrogance that seems earned. He deserved to be the way he was. He had a reputation for nailing the sophomore coeds on the golf course fall and spring, but the reason I didn't like him was not any of this, or because he had a photograph in his dorm room on Alumni Fourth of himself shaking hands with the President, or wore hundred-dollar shoes with no socks to class, but because he hung around our apartment, drinking our tea and chatting—as so many of the Dorcet kids did—with Stacey.

He had always been in our building anyway, picking up a date or lounging in the common room, and then he started dating Rebecca Eastman, the proctor on our floor who was always in our apartment talking to Stacey for hours on end. There was a group of seniors who made our place a nightly rendezvous point: Rebecca and Dalton, another boy named Chip Stewart, two other girls from the floor. Stacey was in law school then and had tales of other worlds. I could hear them in the living room laughing, while I sat in my study and read compositions. Every once in a while I could hear Dalton's polished voice above the rest. Later, I'd go in for more coffee and I'd lean into the room where Dalton would be arranging another log on the fire and ask Rebecca if she didn't have any homework.

"Senior slump," she'd say.

"I've had it for three years," Dalton would say and they'd all laugh again. Paris was three at the time and she'd be walking around with part of a doughnut, printing powered sugar everywhere.

"Come on in," Stacey would say. "We're talking about the First Amendment."

"And the rights of topless dancers," Dalton added.

But I would slip back to my study and pretend to work until the ten o'clock bell sent the boys back to their dorms. Stacey kidded me about being antisocial and a grump. And it was funny; she was right, but there was more.

*ON THE* way to the airport with Paris I asked her if she remembered Dalton.

"Was he at the school?"

"Yes, he used to hold you on his lap and feed you doughnuts."

"That was eons ago. I don't think I remember him." The *eons ago* was one of Stacey's phrases.

"Do you know what an eon is?"

"Six years." She answered with confidence. "Five or six years."

*AT* Dorcet Stacey would sometimes keep the kids after ten if it was a Friday night or the discussion was especially good, some faculty gossip or something. She'd call the other dorm heads and tell them Dalton and Chip would be half an hour late. I remember once coming in for coffee and finding Dalton and Stacey in the kitchen alone. There was nothing going on, but the silence I created by entering the room was so uncomfortable I did an about-face and went back to my work. A moment later Stacey came into the study. "Don't you want to come in and join us?"

"I will," I lied. "As soon as I finish this set of papers."

"Okay," she said. But when she turned to go, I saw something on her rear end. On one cheek of her pants there was a large handprint in powdered sugar. I remember sitting there for an hour, until I heard the boys leave by the front door, and for the whole hour I did not move. I did not close my mouth. All the uneasiness I had about Dalton focused itself sourly.

I never said anything about it. What would I say? Besides it *could* have been *her* handprint. I never did see which side the thumb was on. Later, Dalton arranged to have Stacey's photo in the back of the yearbook captioned *Faculty Fox*. It was a kind of joke, I guess, and when the book came out, we all laughed. I was trying to be large about it, and I kidded Dalton: "She's not on the faculty, Dalton," I said.

His answer: "Hey, sir, but she is a fox, right?"

*EVEN* this late in the spring, the airport was full of skiers from New York. Dalton came striding across that floormap of the world in a blue cashmere blazer and gray slacks. His shirt was open a button or two at the top. He smiled and took my hand, as any young broker should. "Mr. McGuire! Good to see you!" Then he looked at Paris: "And who is this monster? Is this the dear child I rocked on my undergraduate knee?"

Paris did not take his hand. She backed a step and said, "I don't remember you."

He placed a white plastic bag against my belly and whispered, "For you." I looked inside; it was a six-pack of Rolling Rock. "I didn't know if you could get a real brew in this state."

So it all started that night at the Park Cafe. Stacey joined us from the office and she sensed the tension right away. Paris had resisted all of Dalton's good-willed attempts to stir her memories of the old doughnut days. She'd even repeated her *eons ago* line once. I had been matter-of-fact, that is, *cold*, I suppose. He was just too jolly. At one point he had pulled his trouser cuff up to reveal no socks in his new Italian shoes and said, "We're talking vacation here. At the office, it's all socks. There's a dress code just like Dorcet!"

The Park Cafe is not a place to go if you are going with someone who talks too loud. They drywalled the ceiling and no sound escapes, and there was Dalton dropping names at ten decibels. He worked for Parker and Ellis Investment Bankers. He had spent Christmas on St. John's. His father bought a new boat called *The Trickle Down*. Throughout the dinner he called me *Mr. McGuire* and Stacey, *Stacey*. Stacey smiled through all of this, and I simply addressed my pot roast. Paris moved her chair closer to me than usual and talked conspiratorily to me about our plans for this year's kite, which we were planning to make and launch on Saturday.

The next two days, Dalton skied. I drew him a map to Alta, gave him the Honda, and sent him along. The first morning when I handed him the thermos full of coffee, he looked at it as if it were an award and shook his head. "You guys in the west!" he said. "Coffee from a thermos. You guys got it made."

He returned each evening with tales of encounters with young females, describing them as "Narly Madonnas" and describing the conditions as "harsh," a word that in his vocabulary meant *wonderful*. I think. Evenings we'd have *brews* and *suds* and even *brewskis*, and Dalton would say "Hey" a lot in the fashion of the Great White North. He and Stacey would stay up and talk an hour after Paris—and then I—had gone to bed.

When Stacey came to bed after the first night, she turned to me and said, "Be kind, Michael. He looks up to you."

"Sure he does. I married the faculty fox."

"No. Dalton's not doing as well as it seems. He's been deferred from the training program at Parker and Ellis. And Rebecca Eastman, remember?"

"Yeah."

"She just got married in January."

"I'll be kind to him," I said. "I'll try to try harder."

The next night Dalton and Paris and I were all watching the news. One of the leading stories was the weather, a spring storm in Ohio, which everyone was calling the Midwest and which is actually the Mideast, and when Mark Eubank came on, he was his adrenal self. He kept making antic, sweeping gestures and moving around the satellite photograph a lot, like a high school basketball coach in one of his last time outs.

Dalton said: "What is wrong with that guy?"

"He's just our weatherman; he's doing a pretty good job."

Stacey came into the room with some cheese and crackers on the mallard plate my parents gave us a couple of Christmases ago, a plate we hadn't ever—to my knowledge—used. In one hand she had a glass of white wine. "Who's doing a good job?" she said.

"Snowbank," Paris said. "Dalton doesn't like Mr. Snowbank."

Stacey looked at me. "You want some wine?" and then added "Anybody?"

"I'll have a brewski," Dalton said from his deep slump in the butterfly chair. Stacey started back toward the kitchen. "Michael?" she said to me. "Anything for you?"

"No, nothing for me. Thanks."

"No brewski, Dad?" Paris said.

When Stacey had returned with Dalton's can of Rainier and we were watching the sports, she raised her glass and said, "Cheers, everybody. Dalton, we're glad you're here." Paris raised her empty hand and I tapped her knuckles. "And," Stacey went on, saying exactly what I wanted her not to, "tomorrow's Michael's birthday. We'll have to do something special."

"Let's take him skiing with us," Dalton said.

I stared at the footage of Wayne Gretzky scoring from the wing for a moment too long and said, "No, thanks. You two go. Paris and I have plans."

"Birthday kite. Tomorrow we make our kite, right, Dad?"

"Well then, you better get to bed," Stacey said.

"Don't go without a fight, kid," Dalton smiled.

Paris stood. "I don't need to fight," she said. "I've got a big day tomorrow."

"How old will you be?" Dalton turned and gestured to me with his beer can.

"Thirty-seven," I said.

He took a long slug from the beer and then said, "God, I'll bet you're glad it's half over." And he laughed a wit's four-note laugh. I smiled at him. Paris had slipped away.

"Yeah, Dalton," I tried to hold the smile. "It's a relief."

*LATER,* with too much energy to go to bed and not enough stamina to sit up and watch an old *Twilight Zone* on cable with Dalton and Stacey, I prowled around the garage, checking the ski rack and securing their skis for the morning. I climbed up in the pickup bed and pulled three blue bamboo poles from the rafters for our kite, and set them on the workbench. We had about fifty blue and fifty red poles from when I coached the ski team at Dorcet. They were the slalom course one year and when they were all replaced, I kept them for some reason, for this reason, I guess: fifty kites. I looked up. I would be able to make a kite a year until I was almost ninety.

As I put on my pajamas I could hear the television. Dalton's voice came: "What a geek." He was addressing the set. I looked in on Paris and she made that little throaty moan that meant I was supposed to come in and sit for a minute.

"It's going to be a great kite," I said to her. She turned and curled up to me where I sat and put her head alongside my leg. "What's the matter, Paris?" I could see her eyes open, looking hurt. I whispered, "What do you think of Dalton?"

"He's too old to have nicknames for beer." And then she tightened against me and began to cry.

"Paris . . . Paris," I said. "It's okay. You're right, but he's our guest for one more day. We can be nice for one more day, right?"

She nodded against my leg, but the crying intensifed a touch and she clutched me tighter. I leaned down and turned her face into the small light. "Hey, lady," I whispered again. "It's not half over. Dalton was kidding. Your dad's not going anywhere. Do you hear me?"

"He'd miss me too much, wouldn't he?" she said, her lower lip interfering with the words a bit.

"He would." I patted her back and realigned the covers. "He would. You and I are here to stay."

*SATURDAY.* Kite day. My birthday. Dalton was taking a night flight back to New York. Things were going to be all right.

I offered to fry up a quick breakfast for Stacey and Dalton, but Dalton was in a hurry. He was excited to have company for a change and said, "No thanks, Mr. McGuire. We've got to hit the slopes. Let's just stop and get a coffee and some doughnuts at the Seven-Eleven, okay, Stacey?"

"Okay," she said. "Are you sure you two don't want to come with us?"

"Mom," Paris answered. "We've got a kite to build. It's going to take all day."

"Have fun," Stacey said, leaning to kiss me.

"You too," I said. "And Stacey," I pointed at her. "Keep your arms folded."

She shook her head at me as if to say *you sad old fool*, and she and Dalton drove away.

Our kite did take us all day because of material problems. We

143

made the bamboo crossbar in an hour, notching the string sets at each tip and measuring it all with a precision it may not have required. It was a perfect five by three foot cross. But there was no string left from last year, and then I remembered using it on the tomato plants, and the visquine we had planned to use as the sail itself was marred with brown paint. Someone had used it as a dropcloth. So Paris and I ruined the midday cruising Grand Central (now Fred Meyer), Skaggs (now Osco), and ending up at a reliable standby, The West Side Drug Store, which under new management had just been painted blue, which anyone with any sense of history could see was wrong. I hated all the changes. Fred Meyer! And Skaggs, oh please: *Osco?* That sounds like a bad penny stock. But finding the golden drugstore of my youth painted blue, that hurt like a personal insult. Even so, they had four dusty rolls of sturdy kite string, obviously left over from the old days. And the visquine we found at Ketchums, which is also on its way down, but I'm not going to discuss that. By the time we had a late lunch at LaFrontera and had bowed the kite with string, faced the bow with plastic and trimmed it clean, it was after four P.M.

Paris stood up, and the kite was taller than she by a foot. Through the clear plastic, her blurred image appeared to be underwater. "It's beautiful, Dad," she said. "It's so big it won't need a tail, right?"

"Right," I said. We'd learned that lesson last year.

We were both anxious to fly it, but decided to wait until the skiers returned and then take everybody down to Liberty Park for a trial.

Stacey and Dalton pulled in at about five-thirty, sun-burned and exhilarated. "Whoa! Get back!" Dalton called to me. "This woman is harsh! She is totally denied amateur status! Hand her the trophy now and let's have a brew!" He passed me on the way to the fridge. "She can ski!"

Stacey came up the stairs. "We had fun," she said. "It was a little slushy this afternoon, but we had fun."

"Mom, we've got the kite. Let's go down to Liberty Park. We'll all go and fly it!"

"Let me take a quick shower and we'll do that. We can pick up some burgers on the way down, okay, Dalton?"

"Sounds good," he said. "I'm buying. My plane isn't until nine. I'd like to see this kite."

While Stacey was in the shower, Dalton said, in a quiet sober voice I hadn't heard before, "New York is such a grind. I hate to go back." He punched softly at me. "You guys in the west have got it made. All right if I have another beer?"

*LIBERTY PARK* has its beginnings in April. It begins to fill with park people. The young men who polish their cars in groups. The sunbathers in pairs on pastel towels. All the sensible couples walking two dogs on two leashes, marching the perimeter. People play tennis in street clothes, and groups of skeptical children give the playgrounds a first try.

We arrived at the park as the sun was closing in on the Great Salt Lake. I wasn't worried about the time: twilight was longer every evening and I wanted the breezes. The wind was south, so we decided to stage from the big new hill north of the pond. There was only one couple on the far side, making out on a blanket. "Don't look, Mother," Paris laughed. Stacey and Dalton sat halfway up the hill with our white paper bags of sandwiches and fries and that six pack of Rolling Rock, which I had saved for my birthday. Paris and I went down to the level ground and set up.

The breeze was small but steady, and on the first try when Paris released the transparent kite, it held in the air and then rose, slowly, taking string as I backed up.

"Don't you need a tail?" Dalton called.

"No!" Paris yelled back. "We know about that!"

Paris took the controls while I was busy tying the second roll of string to the first.

As the two of us backed, step by step up the hill, the kite now out over the pond two hundred feet, we passed slowly by Dalton and Stacey. He handed me one of the cold Rolling Rocks and said, "Looks good, chief. This Bud's for you."

"It's perfect," Paris corrected him.

We let out the second roll of string and I tied on the third. From the top of the hill we could see the sunset through the trees. The kite was out over a hundred yards. We sat down and began letting out string on the third roll.

"Let's send a message, Dad."

"Okay. Go get a pencil and paper from Mom." Paris ran down fifty yards to where Dalton and Stacey were talking. From where I sat they looked like any other young couple in the park, their shoulders almost touching. I wondered if they'd held arms on the lift. Stacey did that. She held your arm on the lift and laughed and bumped your head softly with hers as you talked on the way up.

Paris returned with a pencil and part of paper sack. It was getting dark, and I had tied on the fourth and last roll of string.

"What are you going to send?" I asked her.

"Is Dalton Mom's boyfriend?" I looked at Paris, but she was looking down at them in the thickening twilight. Their muted voices floated up to us. The transparent kite was getting hard to see. The pull was even and steady as it took the last of the string. A glint from the shiny plastic blinked at us every few seconds.

"Write your message," I said. "It's getting late."

Paris bent to her lap and pressed some words onto the white sheet.

"Here, let me tear it so it will slide," I said, but she held the message back. "I won't look at it." She handed it to me and I tore a slit in the center. "Now fit it onto the string and walk it out a little ways." Paris stood and set the paper on the string and pushed it away about twenty feet, pulling the string down as she went. When she released the cord, it bopped up and her white note began to hop and slide up the inclined line.

"What did it say?" I asked.

"It wasn't to you," she said.

When the message went over Stacey's head, I saw her point up to it. She turned on an elbow and called, "What does it say, Paris?"

"It wasn't to you!" She had the kite string in her hand and bobbed it to help the white sheet ascend. The pull on the increased distance had become powerful as we let out the last fifty feet of string. I tied a stick to the end and she held that as we stared at what we now couldn't see at all. Below us in the dark, Stacey and Dalton had merged into one shadow grouping. A moment later I heard Stacey call: "We better head to the airport, Michael. Paris, are you ready?"

"Really?" Paris whispered to me.

"Yeah." She started to reel in, but I stopped her. "There isn't time, hon." I looked at her as a secret accomplice and whispered: "Let's cut the string!"

Her face went secret and excited. "Okay," she said. "Okay, what do we do?"

I took the stick from her and felt the tremendous pressure of our kite two hundred yards up there somewhere. I handed her my pocketknife and pointed to the string. She nodded slowly, seriously, and pressed the knife to the string. She drew the knife an inch and I felt the line go dead. "Listen," I said. We were both staring furiously into the dark sky. We heard, of course, nothing.

"Where is it, Dad? Is it coming down?" She took my hand.

"That kite won't come down in Utah. That kite is on its way."

*STACEY* did not go to the airport with us. When we arrived home, she got a call from Brokaw at the firm, seven-thirty on Saturday night, and after five minutes, she covered the receiver and said—as she's done before from some new region of seriousness—"It's going to be an hour . . . minimum." So we gathered Dalton's bags and packed the car. Stacey covered the phone again and gave Dalton a hug. She said, "Take care. We loved having you. Good luck."

It was the scene at the airport that came to me a new way. We walked Dalton to his gate. Paris was stopped at security. They discovered my knife in her pocket, and I explained that she was a member of the Swiss Army. The woman smiled but kept the knife for our exit.

At the gate, they were boarding already, and Dalton turned to shake my hand. He looked different. "Thank you for having me," he said. "I know it was kind of a pain. You guys are busy and everything. But you, you were my favorite teacher and, oh hell, I may probably not stay at Parker and Ellis. Econ might have been a mistake for me." He paused and let go of my hand and said: "Happy birthday, sir. I'm not like you, but," and here he looked down to Paris and said to her: "I'm sorry you don't like me, Paris. I won't always be a jerk." He looked back into my face and smiled. "*I won't.* Thanks a lot. Good-bye."

We retrieved the pocket knife and on the way home Paris asked, "What are you thinking, Dad?"

I put my hand on her head and told the perennial, the ancient lie: "Nothing, honey." What I was thinking was this: I had wanted to settle. I wanted to hold on to my superiority and settle. Dalton. He had confused this old fool. I had seen Paris's message to the kite and it had said: "Please don't let Dalton be Mom's boyfriend." And I had been less than friendly to this boy who had flown across the country to see his old teacher. I had defended Mark Eubank, of all things.

I shook my head as we moved left to take the City Center Exit. We were going home. It was the second half of my life. I would have to do better.

# MILK

*THEY* almost fingerprint the children before I can stop them. Phyllis is making a rare personal appearance in my office to help me with a motorcycle injury claim, and I want to squeeze every minute out of her, and I'm taking no calls. We all call Phyllis "The Queen of Wrongful Death," which is the truest nickname in the firm. She likes being a hard case, and she's lording it over me a bit this morning, rereading a lot of the stuff that I'd summarized for her, when Tim buzzes and says Annie's on the line.

I almost wave it off. She probably wants to meet for lunch and today there's going to be no lunch, because I want to get this motorcycle case buttoned up so we can take the twins on a picnic this weekend. Now that they can walk, our house is getting real small. But it's not lunch. Annie's voice is down a note or two, stern, as she says she and my mother are going to take the boys down to Community Fuel, where there is another fingerprint program today. I listen to Annie tell the story and watch Phyllis frowning through the file. My mother read about the program in the paper and with so many children abducted and missing, etc. etc. etc. Annie closes with *I know what you think, but this is something we should do for your mother's sake.*

I don't say anything.

"Jim?" Annie says.

"Ann. You said it. You know what I think. *No way*. Not the twins. Not for my mother. Not for anybody."

"She's coming over to get us in half an hour."

"Ann," I say again. "Take her to lunch, but do not fingerprint the boys. Okay? Under no circumstances. That's all."

"It's no big deal . . ."

"Tell my mother that."

"I'm going to tell your mother that you're terrified and unable at this time to do the right thing."

When I hang up, Phyllis looks up. At thirty-four she wears those imperious half glasses, which, in a drunken moment at the firm barbeque last summer, she admitted to me are just part of her costume, "dress to win"; and I admit now that they intimidate me.

"Fingerprints?" she says. "Are the twins being booked?"

"It's that I.D. program at Community Fuel. My mother wants to take the kids."

"And . . .?"

"My kids are not being fingerprinted. I'm not caving in to this raging paranoia. It's a better world than people think."

Phyllis takes off her awful glasses and lets them drop on their necklace against her breast. "And you're not scared in the least, are you?"


*WHEN* I come home from work, Lee and Bobby laugh their heads off. It has become my favorite part of the day. I peek into the kitchen and say, "Oh-oh!" and they amble in stiffly in their tiny overalls, arms up for balance. They start: "Oh-oh!" as I pick them up and they laugh and laugh as we do our entire repertoire of sounds: *Dadda, Momma, Baby,* and the eleven or twelve other syllables, as well as a good portion of growling, humming, meow-ing, mooing, and buzzing. When I whistle softly through my teeth, they hug me hard to make me stop.

They are fraternal twins. Bobby has a lot of hair and a full face. Lee, though he probably weighs the same, twenty-two pounds, seems slighter, more fragile. Ironically, Bobby cries more and easier. They can lie on a blanket with fists full of each other's hair, and only Bobby will fuss. They each have four and a half teeth and they call each other the same name: *Baby*.

Tonight I lift them up and the laughing intensifies as I tote them into the living room where Annie is picking up the blanket and toys.

She starts right in: "Well, boys, it's Daddy, the Rulemaker."

"Annie . . ."

"The lawgiver." She holds the bundle in her arms and stands to face me. She goes on in a gruff voice: "*No fingerprints. Not in this house! Not for anybody!*"

Bobby and Lee think this is wonderful and they laugh again. Each has a good hold on my hair and their laughing pulls my scalp in two directions. Annie comes right up to the boys and makes a mock frown, her nose against mine. She growls. "*Not even for my mother!*" She kisses me quickly and disappears into the boys' room. The boys snap around to watch her and the hair pulling brings tears to my eyes.

Annie's got me. We've been married nine years, and it's been a good marriage. We've grown up together really, and only since the boys have arrived have I started with this rule stuff. Annie and I used to go crazy after visiting our friends Stuart and Ruth and their kids. Everything was rules. *No baseball in the backyard. No jackets in the basement. No magazines in the kitchen. No loud talking in hall. No snacks during homework.* We promised then never to post rules. Driving home from their house, Annie and

I would make up rules and laugh until we'd have to pull over. *No hairdryers in the bathtub. No looking out the window while someone is talking to you. No peeking at the answers to the crossword puzzle. No shirt, no shoes, no service.* And Annie even gave Ruth one of our ridiculous lists, typed up as a joke (their lists were typed and posted on the refrigerator door), but Ruth did not think it was that funny. She said, "Wait until you have kids."

And now I have both kids in my arms when Annie comes back into the room. "Call your mother," she says, taking Lee from me and putting him in his high chair. "She wants to know why you're not looking out for the best interest of your children. Put Bobby in his chair before you call, okay?"

*WE'VE* been through this all before, but I can see this week is going to be worse. I watched the news programs on television and saw the troops of children being fingerprinted. I made it clear from the beginning that we did not want to do that. Annie watched my opposition grow over the weeks, realizing that this was probably the biggest disagreement in our marriage.

"I don't understand you," she said. "You're a lawyer, for Petes' sakes. You like things nailed down. What's the problem?"

But she said it as: what's *your* problem? I watched the children, many babies, being fingerprinted. I couldn't express what my problem was.

And my mother wanted to know why, in light of all the missing children and the recent abductions, why wouldn't I do it *for their sake.*

"Because," I had explained to her at last, at the end of my patience: "Because the only use those prints will ever have is in identifying *a body*, okay? *Do you see?* They use them to identify the body. And my children will not need fingerprints, *because nothing is going to happen to my children.* Is that clear?" I had almost yelled at my mother. "We don't need fingerprints!"

Then my mother would be hurt for a few days and then silent for a few days, and then there'd be another news story and we'd do it all again.

Annie tried to intervene. "Stop being a jerk. It's not a big deal. It's not going to hurt the boys. They'll forget it. Your mother would feel better."

"No."

"Why not?"

I don't know how many times we had some version of that conversation, but I do know that once I took Annie's wrist and raged through the house like the sorry creature I can be at times, pointing to the low surfaces, "Because, we've got fingerprints! Look!" I made her look at the entryway door and the thousand hands printed there, at the car windows, and the front of the fridge, and finally the television, where a vivid hand printed in rice cereal made Tom Brokaw on the evening news look like he was growing a beard. "We have fingerprints. And I love these fingerprints. We don't need any others."

All Annie said was, "Can I have this now?" She indicated her arm. I let her go. She shook her head at me and went in to check on the boys.

*AND* there was the milk.

I wanted Annie to change milk. We had been getting the Hilltop green half-gallon cartons. Then they started putting children on the back panels, missing children. Under the bold heading, MISSING, would be two green and white photographs of the children, their statistics printed underneath: date of birth; age; height; eyes; hair; weight; date missing; from . . . . The photographs themselves assumed a lurid, tabloid quality, and everytime I opened the fridge they scared me. I'd already seen ads for missing children on a weekly mailer we receive which offers—on the flip side—discount coupons for curtain and rug cleaning, optical services, and fast food, primarily chicken. And in Roy's Drug one night I dropped the Archie comic I was going to buy for the boys (to keep them from ripping up our art books), when I saw two missing children inside the front cover. It was all getting to me.

One night late, I went into Smith's Food King and turned all the Hilltop milk to the back panel so sixty children stared out from the dairy case. I started it as a statement of some kind, but when I stepped back across the aisle and saw their group sadness, all those green and white poor resolution smiles, wan even in the bright Food King light, I lost my breath. I fled the store and sulked home and asked Annie if we could buy another brand.

When I told her why, when I told her about the two kids taking a little starch out of the world for me when I opened the refrigerator at two A.M. to grab Bobby a bottle, those nights when he still fusses, Annie just said *No*.

*TONIGHT* after I have the fifteenth version of my fingerprint call with my mother, I am out of tolerance, reason, generosity, and any of their relatives. I never swear in the company of my mother, and as I sit down in the kitchen and watch Annie spoon the boys their macaroni and strained beef, I think perhaps I should. I might not have this knot in my neck. There on the table is the Hilltop milk with somebody's picture on the back.

I don't know why, but I start: "Annie, I don't want this milk in the house."

She's cool. "And is there a reason for that, oh powerful Rule-maker?"

"I've told you the reason. I'm not interested in being depressed or in having my children frightened by faces of lost souls in the refrigerator."

Annie says nothing. She spoons the macaroni into Bobby's open mouth. After each mouthful, he goes: "mmmmnnnnn!" and laughs. It's something I taught the boys with Milupa and bananas, but Lee's version is softer, almost a sigh of satisfaction.

"What is the point? There is no point in publishing these lurid photographs."

"They're not lurid."

"What's the point? I am supposed to study the carton, cruise the city, stop every child walking home from school: *is he missing? would he like to go home now?* Really, what? I see some girl playing tennis against the practice wall in Liberty Park, am I supposed to match her with my carton collection of missing children?" I've raised my voice a little, I can tell, because Annie looks narrow-eyed, stony.

She hands me the spoon for Lee, who is smiling at me for yelling. Annie rises and takes the milk and puts it in the refrigerator. "Missing children don't get to play tennis," she says quietly, wiping Bobby up and putting him on the floor. Bobby goes immediately to the one cupboard I haven't safety clipped, opens it, and pulls a large bottle of olives onto his foot.

He watches the bottle roll across the floor and when it stops against the stove, he looks up into my face with his beautiful face and he starts to cry.

"Bobby's first," Annie says, plucking him from the floor. "Bobby's first in bed tonight!"

When she carts Bobby off, I let Lee out of his chair. I hand him his bottle out of the fridge and he takes it with both hands as if it were an award. He starts to walk off, then realizes, I guess, that Mom isn't here and he doesn't really know where to go. So, he looks up at me, a child who resembles an angel so much it is troubling. Then Annie is behind him, lifting him away, and I am left alone in the kitchen.

I wipe up the chairs and the floor and cap the macaroni and strained beef, but when I put them away, I see that green Hilltop milk carton.

"You want to close the fridge?" Annie is behind me.

"No look. Look at this."

"Close the fridge door."

"Look!" I point at the child, his green and white photograph so grim in the bright light of the fridge.

I take one carton of milk out and close the fridge. I read aloud: "MISSING: Name: Richard Tarrel. D.O.B.: 10/21/82. Age: 4. Height: 2 feet 8 inches. Eyes: blue. Hair: light brown. Weight: 27 pounds. Date missing: 6/24/84. From: Omaha . . . ." I mean to make a point by reading it, but the *twenty-seven pounds* gets me a little, and by the time I read *Omaha*, I stop and sit down and look across at Annie. She looks like she is going to cry. She looks a lot like I have made her cry again.

She firms her mouth once and shakes her head as she stands up to leave the room. "Nebraska," she whispers. "Omaha, Nebraska."


*I SIT* at the kitchen table listening to Bobby and Lee murmuring toward sleep in their room, and I look at little twenty-seven pound Richard Tarrel. Even in the poor quality photograph, he is beautiful, his eyes huge and dark, his lips pouted in a coy James Dean smile. There is no background in the photo, but I've been to Omaha. I can imagine the backyard somewhere out near 92nd Street, the swingset, the young peach tree Richard's father planted this summer, after the man at the nursery told

him that though it was small, there would be peaches next
fall.


*THE* next morning, I've got the day trip to Denver, the quick
deposition, and back on the nine o'clock. Annie is cordial to me
in the morning, well, stern. I have a cup of coffee and pick at
some of Bobby's scrambled eggs. Annie doesn't offer to have the
whole gang drive me to the airport, which would have happened
if we weren't fighting. I feel bad about it, kind of flat, but the
boys will not have their fingerprints taken. I do not believe in
it and it will not happen. Not my boys. It's a rule.

The flight over is rocky. The plane pitches heavily up the slope
and then down, across the mountains to Denver. Sitting in the
window seat of my row, one empty seat away, is a pale blond
girl. I'm trying to fill in all the forms so I can maybe make the
early plane tonight, but she stops me. I have to study her. She
huddles to the window, her fragile face poised there, watching
the unchanging grayness. Her Levis are worn and the red plaid
bag she clutches on her lap is years old. Her shirt is a blue stripe
dress shirt that could have never, ever fit her; it is five sizes large.
She sits in a linty, dark blue serape. I can't stop myself from
looking at her. Date of Birth: 1969. Age: 17; Height: 5'9"; Eyes:
brown; Hair: light blond; Weight: 120; Date Missing: . . . .

The girl turns her face to me in the bouncing airplane and
speaks, her lips barely moving: "Don't," she says. "Please. Just
don't."

My deposition is a witness to a motorcycle accident, a sophomore in psychology, and I meet him at the University Union in
Boulder just after noon. In our hour, I learn: both children moved
to avoid the cycle, but they moved different ways and one, the
victim, our client, was hit and injured. My witness was driving

pizza delivery behind the motorcycle and saw it all. Daylight. Sun to his back. A simple story. After the witness leaves for class, I sit in the modular furniture mesmerized for a while by the young people streaming around me.

There are children everywhere. All the way down the highway from Boulder to Denver, I see them alone and in groups, kicking along in the gravel. They all seem to need haircuts. I check my watch: two o'clock on a school day. Why isn't anybody where he's supposed to be? I think about our case; it's a given. I wonder what help the settlement will be to the parents of the hurt girl. I try to make the equation in my mind. We'll ask for six hundred thousand and get two. The girl's eleven years old and has one complete knee and six-tenths of the other. Let's see: she'll have that limp for sixty-eight years, if she lives her statistic. That's three thousand dollars a year not to walk like everyone else, or play soccer, I guess, or tennis. I ditch my rental car at the Avis curb, and think: what a strange man I'm becoming. What's happening to me?

The six o'clock is full so I hit the little sky-lounge near the gate and have a Manhattan. I used to love having an hour or two to ransack the magazines and have a Manhattan, my little joke living in the West, but now it's not much fun. There seem somes urgency about getting home. I can't really settle down. I want to get home.


*SOMETIMES*, driving home alone in the last two blocks before our house, a feeling descends upon me like a gift. It is as if a huge door opens and I can breathe differently, see the entire scope of our lives, and it makes me unreasonably happy. It makes me want to rush into the kitchen and sweep Annie up and cry: *forgive me, forgive us, let's never quarrel again, we have everything*. I don't know where the feeling comes from or how real it is, but I have it tonight as I turn into the driveway.

My mother's white Seville is parked to one side, something I didn't really want to see, but there's our house standing like a house in a story, an entire happy little world. The kitchen windows are beautiful yellow squares and a blue glow in the two small windows out front means they're watching television.

I vow to go in cheerfully and join them, open a beer, chat openly with the two women about everything. This fingerprint thing doesn't have to be such a big deal. We can agree. We can face the future without unreasonable fear.

In the kitchen, two blue Community Fuel Folders spill across the table. On the cover of each is a large white fingerprint the size of a head of lettuce. Underneath the print, it says: COMMUNITY I.D. / PROJECT FINGERPRINT. I can hear the women talking in the other room under the television noises. I open the first folder and there it is in Annie's printing: Bobby Hensley. Date of Birth. Age. Weight. Hair. There is an empty square: place recent photograph here. And below: the ten smudges of Bobby's fingers.

I reach two bottles out of the fridge, one Nuk, one yellow nipple for Lee, and slip them inside my sportcoat. I tiptoe into the boys' room. Lee is asleep in a knot of blanket; Bobby lies on his side with his thumb loosely in his mouth experimenting with sounds: *doya, doya, moya*. He looks up at me calmly and smiles and then rolls to a crawl and stands in his crib. I pick him up and park him in a shoulder and then lift Lee like a melon under my forearm. I sweep the boys noiselessly through the kitchen and out to the car.

I calm enough to strap them in their car seats, Lee asleep in the back and Bobby on the seat next to me in the front. I coast back down the driveway before starting the car, and I am on the road half a block before I pull the lights on.

"Ba," Bobby says as we pass a city bus in front of East High. "Ba."

"Bus," I say, the first word I've said aloud since my plane landed. "That's right. It's a bus."

The streets are luminous, wet and shiny, ticketed with early leaves, and our tires make the friction I have always loved to hear after rain. So the streets whisper darkly as we slow at each bright intersection, the flaring Seven-Elevens, the flat white splash of a gas station. Then it is dark again, and we are driving.

Lee starts to squeak, which means he will babble for a while and then cry. He's a little tongue-tied and is gradually tearing the cord underneath by stretching his mouth in low squalls which becomes real crying after about a minute. I stop at the light at Fourth and State and give both boys their bottles.

We turn left onto State and head south, cruising by the jillion colored lights the kids love. In the rearview mirror, I can see Lee settled now in his seat. He has learned to balance the bottle on the carseat arm-tray, so his hands are free. Right now, they extend off to each side, palms up, and Lee opens and closes his hands slowly as he watches them and sucks on the bottle.

Bobby has his head tipped right to witness the spectacle of neon from the bars and motels, the bright dragon above the Double Hey Rice Palace, the pulsing tire in front of Big O. He has his bottle clutched in both hands and set hard in the side of his mouth like a cigar.


WHEN I was a boy I remember that my father would always pick up babies in restaurants. We'd go to Harmon's on North Temple about every other Sunday as a treat. My brother and I always had the gorgeous shakes, strawberry and chocolate, too thick for the straw, my mother always wore one of her three pretty dresses and patted our faces with the corner of her napkin, and my father would always spot a baby three tables away. He would simply rise and go over to the little family and pick up their baby and bring it over to our table and talk to it, asking did it want to be ours and things like that, just loud enough for the parents to hear. I remember the parents always smiling, perhaps an older sister craning her neck to see where the baby had gone, and my father dipping a spoon into my strawberry shake for the child. Sometimes he'd keep the baby on his lap for half an hour, showing off, sometimes, he would return it right away, the baby squirming in his arms, fighting for a last glance at my strawberry shake. My father gave forty kids their first taste of ice cream at our table, and no one seemed to be scared of anything.

"*NAMMA,*" Bobby says, lifting his bottle over the seat and dropping it. He places one hand on the window and says it again, "Namma."

Somewhere out in this garish Disneyland of light, he has spotted a bear, and now he wants "Namma," his bear, actually a stuffed toy raccoon. Namma is the one who taught us all *peek-a-boo* and *Where's-your-nose*. In my haste leaving the house, I have forgotten Namma.

In the backseat, Lee is again asleep, his arms limp at his sides, his bottle still protruding from his mouth.

"Namma," Bobby says, turning to me.

"Namma," I say back to him, and he smiles. We will have to go home. Namma is at home peeking out of a corner of the crib. Bobby is still smiling at me coyly, waiting for me to say something else, so I sing his favorite song: "The Lion Sleeps Tonight."

"Ooh Wimoweh. Wimoweh, O Wimoweh . . ." I sing, nodding my head so Bobby will nod his too. "In the jungle, the quiet jungle, the lion sleeps tonight. . . ."

# MILK

Tired, he leans his head back against the car seat and watches me sing, his open-mouth grin never changing. I do a lot of extra "*O Wimoweh's*," and the song ends somewhere in Murray. Bobby has closed his mouth now; his eyes are next. I look at my watch: ten to twelve; and I realize that this is the latest I've been out since the boys were born, and people are everywhere. We better go home.

I do a U-turn in the bright, crowded parking lot of a Seven-Eleven. A lone teenager leans against the phones, smoking a cigarette. He wears a Levi jacket and a blue bandanna around his neck. I look at his face, the eyebrows almost grown together, the pretty lower lip. Date of Birth: 1971; Age: 15; Height: 5'7"; Weight: 125; Eyes: blue; Hair: dark brown; Date missing: I don't know. On the milk carton there will be a date, but as I glance back at the boy, I can only see that it looks like he's been out in the night a long time.

Three blocks later, Bobby's asleep. It's late. The traffic is thick and bright. I pass a twenty-four hour Safeway and the parking lot is full. Behind me the headlights teem. A man cruises by us smoking a cigarette in a large Chevrolet. Two couples on motorcycles, the girls holding on, their faces turned out of the wind into their boyfriends' backs. A new station wagon, three girls bouncing in the front seat. Two boys in a Volkswagen bug, their elbows out the window as if summer weren't really over.

At home Annie has checked on the children by now and found them gone, and she has found my valise, and she has given my mother another drink and calmed her down. She knows I'm coming home. We have been safe all our lives. We've traveled: London, Tokyo, Paris, where we saw a diplomat shot down the block from us. Annie has broken her leg skiing. Our Cherokee was totaled by a street department truck two summers ago. We have always felt safe until the boys arrived, and now I am afraid of everything.

I start to sing. We're locked in, the windows are up. These are my boys. I sing softly: "Ooh Wimoweh. Wimoweh, O Wimoweh, Wimoweh," and on, even at a stoplight. I can feel people looking at me, and I lower my face onto the back of my hand on the steering wheel. It's so late. What is everybody doing up so late?

# BLOOD

## AND ITS RELATIONSHIP

## TO WATER

*THE* noise Eddie makes when he first wakes for his two A.M. feeding is closest to a fanbelt slipping, a faint periodic squealing, which like a loose fanbelt doesn't signal an emergency; it just means that if not looked to soon, there is going to be real trouble. In Eddie's case, if we linger in our bed too long, the sound becomes a wail similar to that of straining power steering in some late-model Fords. Some Fairlane will try a U-turn on a side street and you hear that low scream near the front axle.

At six weeks, Eddie's also developing a strange growl that he uses primarily when we try to burp him; it is as if he's trying to fake one so as to get back to the bottle. And at night sometimes, as the fanbelt slips into the power steering wail, he'll throw in a little growl as counterpoint, just to show us he's beginning to do things on purpose.

He also has a four-note nasal coo, which is the sweetest noise ever created. He coos whenever the bottle is plugged in his mouth, and sometimes he coos for a moment or two after he's eaten, as his eyes roll sleepily back in his lids.

We know his every peep, every soft snort (he has two), and we listen to him and study these noises because like any parents, we take them as signs of life. We go to the crib at all hours and listen for the feather breath, the muted sigh, some small sound.

But we are also keen because Nancy is looking for a sign of love. She hangs on his every glance, tic, start; he's smiled a couple of times now and when he has, Nancy has called me into the room where she stands with his little head in her hands, while she sobs and sobs. "He smiled," she says. "He smiled at me." She has fallen in love with Eddie so profoundly that our house seems a new place, and she needs some small sign of love in return.

I know she's going to get one, but she is not so sure. Eddie came to our house in the arms of my lawyer's wife, Bonnie, when he was two days old. Bonnie, who has four children of her own, was weeping, and repeating again and again: "He's so beautiful, so perfect." It was the moment of transfer that changed Nancy, utterly. She had been cool. She had been hopeful, surely, but also steady and reasonable, and then when Bonnie put Eddie in Nancy's arms, it was as if the infant carried 50,000 volts of some special electricity. Nancy sat down with her eyes on his little face, and her mouth became a scared line. I stood there wishing she would just cry instead of looking like she was about to start crying.

And it's been that way for six weeks. A solemnity has crept into our lives as my wife, the dearest soul I know, waits to see if this adopted child will love her. Hey, I've talked to her, and obviously, logic has no place in the deal. So my wife listens to the baby and watches his face the way astronomers stare into the deepest heavens for the first sign of a new star.

*TONIGHT*, when Sam came over, in fact, was the first time Nancy has relaxed enough to drink a beer, and I think by the time he left after midnight, she'd had four. Sam loves kids and just the way he held Eddie and how obviously happy he is for us to have a baby put Nancy at ease.

I brought a chair in from the dining room and we sat in the kitchen and Sam tried to remember when Robbie and Juney were babies. He told a funny story about how Rob wouldn't stop crying at night and the doctor had told them just to let him cry. But a neighbor, suspecting child abuse, had called the police. It had happened twice. Now Robbie is fifteen and works for me weekends, mowing the lawn and washing the cars. He lives with his mother.

After his ten o'clock bottle, Eddie went to bed, bunching himself on his arms and knees like a bug. When I returned to the kitchen, Nancy had opened another beer and had her feet up under herself on the chair. Sam had opened the window and pulled out his cigarettes. Something was up.

Well, with our old friend Sam, it's always Vicky. They've been divorced over three years, but he feels that she still conducts her life around a massive and undiminished hatred for him. "It's no Sun Valley this summer," he said, blowing smoke like a strong secret out the window. He smokes differently since we've gotten the baby. "It's her option, as always, and she says that she and Jeff are taking the kids to San Diego for five weeks after the Fourth. She's known since Thanksgiving about my time off and my plans to let Juney learn to ride, but all of a sudden, she's got this craving to take the kids on her honeymoon. Rob and Juney are acting funny, like it was my fault, like if I'm really their father why don't I just make it happen."

Sam lifted an empty beer can and deposited his cigarette, tilting the can to extinguish the butt. I remember Vicky smirking when he did that; she always called him a "bo-ho," her joke for *bohemian*.

"Rob sure is getting to be a handsome young man," Nancy said.

"Now that is undisguised flattery," I said to Sam. "He looks just like you." And Rob does. What is most affecting, however, is that Rob *walks* just like Sam, and when we play one on one in the driveway, Rob has the same fake-left-go-right move that Sam uses. I haven't told him about it yet, because with my age, I need the little advantage.

"I wonder if Eddie will look like us," Nancy said, hugging her knees in her chair.

"He already does," Sam said. "The poor little guy has that problem already." He reached for his cigarettes, showed them to us. "How we doing with the smoke?"

"You're all right, Sam. None's blowing in here," Nancy said.

"I look more like my father than my brother Tim does," Sam said, lighting up and shaking the match in front of the window opening. "Tim's even six inches shorter than both of us." He laughed. "I think it pisses him off."

"It sure forced him to become an outside shooter," I said. I reached behind Nancy into the fridge. "Beer?"

"One more, then I gotta go," Sam said. "Last hearing on the rate hike tomorrow; the public defender better be sharp."

"Tim's not adopted," Nancy said, taking the beer from me. "Is he?"

"No. He and Irene came along after Mom and Dad had adopted me and Carrie."

I took a chance. "Nancy's a little worried, Sam." I said. "How . . ."

"How do you feel about *your* parents?" Nancy said.

Sam looked up, his face confused, and then he looked over at Nancy, huddled on her chair. His face rose into a large grin. "You're kidding," he said. "Nan, you're worried? Come on. She's kidding, right?" Sam leaned on his elbows toward Nancy. "Well, don't worry. He's your little boy and he'll always be your boy. Look at me. I love my parents and I love my kids; it's my wife

I can't abide." Sam laughed and stuck the cigarette back in his mouth. "She's the one who grew up to hate me."

Sam stood up. "I gotta go. Thanks for the beer. I'll call you late tomorrow and give you the play by play of the hearing."

"What will you do if you can't take the kids to Sun Valley?"

"Plan two. Stay around here. Drink beer with you guys. Teach Eddie about women and how to ride a bike."

"Go on," Nancy said. "You're not finished. What's the punchline?"

Sam shrugged and opened the door. "Once you learn to ride a bike, you never forget."

After Sam left I asked Nancy if she felt better.

"Sam's a good guy," she said. "And I should probably drink more beer; this is the first time my back has let go since the baby got here."

"What about this. You go to bed and I'll listen for the baby," I said, clearing the counter.

"My son," she smiled briefly hugging me, her head against my chest. "Please listen for my son."


I T was twelve minutes after two when the fanbelt began to squeal, just a short touch and then another, then the real sound of a fanbelt slipping. I mean, it is so close I could tape it and convince people of car trouble. Nancy was out so cold with the worry and fatigue of six weeks that in the half light we have from the hall she could have been the definitive photograph of sleep deprivation.

You see a kid that small in his crib and it looks like someone sleeping on a jailhouse floor and you don't wonder about *any* sound he may make. I slipped my hand under Eddie's head just as the fanbelt was rising into power steering trouble and we ducked quickly into the kitchen. He quieted for the ride into the new room, and the quick flash from the fridge door turned his head in curiosity for the moment that allowed me to retrieve the bottle and stick it in the warmer. Since we'd had the baby, I'd become used to standing naked in the kitchen at night with Eddie in my arms.

The standing-zombie fatigue was worst the third week and now in the sixth it had settled to just my eyes and knees, a low burning. My head rocked slightly and I kept my eyes closed, drifting through the routine.

While Eddie was still too amazed at being whisked around to cry, I changed him, and when I pulled the heavy wet diaper away from under him, he swam happily in the air for a moment, punching softly into the dark. By the time I had him powdered and diapered, he was squealing again, each breath a wonderful, powerful compression, focused and building.

In the kitchen, the bottle was ready. I found it without reaching twice, unplugging the warmer as an afterthought, the kind of motion that in ten years I would forget I had committed a thousand times. With a quick flip I had milk on my wrist, and then of all the easy connections and coincidences in the universe, the baby's mouth found the nipple easiest of all. And as I walked around my own house naked as they say Adam was, holding my son, I heard cooing, edged by a kind of purring slurp, and one or two real, honest deep breaths.

In the dark living room, I sat in the corner of the old couch, holding Eddie and listened until he snorted two or three times and then gasped, a sharp little gasp, and I knew that two ounces were down, and we could try for a little air. I stood him against my chest and patted his back while he squirmed and growled, his head bobbing in search of the bottle. Then he grew quiet, which always is a good sign. He stood, head away from my body, as if he was listening for something, and then it came: a belch, a good two-stage belch, which he delivered partially in my ear and which sounded exactly like a lawn mower coming around the corner of a house. After that, his head bobbed some more, poking me about the face, and he was ready for more dinner.

I had already fallen asleep twice during the feeding, but sometime during the second burping, Eddie really woke me up with his head. He was bumping against my face softly, working his mouth like a little fish, whining a little bit, when I felt him swing back into space. I had a good hold of him, so I wasn't too worried, when *wham*! his forehead hammered my nose. I saw a quick flash and my eyes filled with tears that burned and burned. I must have started or moved somehow, because I felt Eddie wet me right through the diaper leg, which—out of a kind of misguided concern—I always leave a little loose.

Eddie was fussing and I stood and walked him around the room for a minute, too tired to change him, too tired to go to bed. My head felt strange, kind of empty. And finally I gave up in the middle of our second lap and sat back on the couch. Leaning there I burned with fatigue, wet and warm, and headed toward three o'clock.

Once or twice I thought about getting up, drying us off, and going back to bed, but my head was light and I was tired to the bone. Eddie began to sleep there on my chest, evenly against me, each breath a bird wing in the night sky. I pulled the T.V. quilt over us and leaned back into warm sleep myself.

It's funny about love, about how you think you're in love or how you may think you know your capacity for love, and suddenly somebody like Eddie comes along and shows you whole new rooms in your heart. I never thought Nancy would be nervous about making this baby belong to us; and when I saw that she was, that she wanted fiercely for him to be ours in every way, I started getting nervous, because I didn't know how to help her.

When I woke there was crying. This was no gentle revving

of the small engines of crying. This was roaring, and then I opened my eyes and it was Nancy. She had a hand on my forehead and all I could see in her face was her open mouth in a gasp so full of horror and fear as to seem counterfeit. Her eyes were wide, crystalline, unblinking. In the late dawn light, she looked as though she had bad news for me.

Then I looked down. Eddie lay on my chest in a thick mess which included the blanket, both my hands, my side, and a good portion of the couch cushion. It was blood. I reached up and felt the crust of blood on my neck and chin. My head ached slowly, a low-grade ice-cream headache, and I felt my swollen nose with my fingers. All the time, I realized, my other hand had been feeling Eddie sleep.

"It's okay, Nan," I said in a thick voice. "I had a bloody nose." She sat on her heels next to me, her hands now clasped in her lap, her lower lip clipped fast in her teeth. "Eddie's okay. He's still sleeping, see?" I tried to lift Eddie up just a little to show his breathing face to her, and when I tried that, I realized we were stuck. My nose had bled over everything, blood that would be on the couch for generations, and now a thin layer of blood had glued Eddie to my belly and chest.

When you lie naked in an empty bathtub with your son attached to your abdomen by the stickiness of your very blood, and your wife gingerly sponges you apart with lukewarm water, there is a good chance you too will wake the baby. Eddie opened his eyes in the warm wash of water and lifted his head, as he's learning to do. His eyes tracked the strange space, while Nancy squeezed water between us, and then he saw his mother and made the most extraordinary gesture of tilting his head in recognition, his mouth pursing comically as if to say, *Please, Mom, spare me this indignity.*

And she did. With a noise of her own, something between a

sigh and a cough, Nancy reached down for her child. His body awash with blood and water, Eddie hopped into his laughing mother's arms. There was no question about it this time: he put his arms around her laughing neck and, in a happy, bucking hug, he grabbed her hair.

# MAX

*MAX* is a crotch dog. He has powerful instinct and insistent snout, and he can ruin a cocktail party faster than running out of ice. This urge of his runs deeper than any training can reach. He can sit, heel, fetch; he'll even fetch a thrown snowball from a snowfield, bringing a fragment of it back to you delicately in his mouth. And then he'll poke your crotch, and be warned: it is no gentle nuzzling.

So when our friend Maxwell came by for a drink to introduce us to his new girlfriend, our dog Max paddled up to him and jabbed him a sharp one, a stroke so clean and fast it could have been a boxing glove on a spring. Maxwell, our friend, lost his breath and sat on the couch suddenly and heavily, unable to say anything beyond a hoarse whisper of *"Scotch.* Just *scotch.* No ice."

Cody put Max out on the back porch, of course, where he has spent a good measure of this long winter, and Maxwell took a long nourishing sip on his scotch and began recovering. He's not athletic at all, but I admired the way he had folded, crumpling just like a ballplayer taking an inside pitch in the nuts. It wasn't enough to change my whole opinion of him, but it helped me talk to him civilly for five minutes while Cody calmed the dog. I think I had seen a sly crocodile smile on Max's face after he'd struck, pride in a job well done, possibly, and then again, possibly a deeper satisfaction. He had heard Cody and me talk about Maxwell before, and Max is a smart dog.

Maxwell, his color returning, was now explaining that his new girlfriend, Laurie, would be along in a minute; she had been detained at aerobics class. Life at the museum was hectic and lovely, he was explaining. It was frustrating for him to be working with folk so ignorant of what made a good show, of counterpoint, of even the crudest elements of art. Let alone business, the business of curating, the business of public responsibility, the business in general. I was hoping to get him on his arch tirade about how the average intelligence in his department couldn't make a picture by connecting the dots, a routine which Cody could dial up like a phone number. But I wasn't going to get it tonight; he was already on business, his favorite topic.

The truth is that Maxwell is a simple crook. He uses his office to travel like a pasha; he damages borrowed work, sees to the insurance, and then buys some of it for himself; he only mounts three shows a year; and he only goes in four days a week.

Cody came in for one of her favorite parts, Maxwell's catalogue (including stores and prices) of the clothing and jewelry he was wearing tonight. Cody always asked about the clerks, and so his glorious monologue was sprinkled with diatribes about the help. Old Maxwell.

When his girlfriend, Laurie, finally did arrive, breathless and airy at the same time, Maxwell had all three rings on the coffee table and he was showing Cody his new watch. Laurie tossed her head three times taking off her coat; we were in for a record evening.

Maxwell would show her off for a while, making disparaging remarks about exercise *of any kind*, and she would admire his rings, ranking them like tokens on the table, going into complex and aesthetic reasons for her choices. I would fill her full of the white wine that all of Maxwell's girlfriends drink, and then when she asked where the powder room was, I would rise with her and go into the kitchen, wait, count to twenty-five while selecting another Buckhorn out of the fridge, and let Max in.

# THE
# STATUS QUO

*IT* was a tough time and she didn't know why. One of those times that *develops* like a storm front, slowly, imperceptibly; you run to the store a few times, drive your boys to piano and tennis for a few years, and suddenly you look up and something's tough, *something* hurts.

Changes had already begun before Glenna saw Jim in the tub. She's already changed radio stations, switching from KALL and its forced adult glee to somplace in the sevens, a station she didn't even know the name of that played raw, vaguely familiar rock and roll. And she played it loudly, driving around in the Volvo. Glenna would come out of Seven-Eleven with a coffee and she could hear the music vibrating the running car. And she found herself going to movies alone in the afternoon. One day she went to see *Micki and Maude* at the Regency and though she knew it was one of the worst pictures she had ever seen, she couldn't help feeling for the characters, losing herself in the wash of images. On the way home, she stopped at the Upper Crust and had a cup of cappuccino sitting in the corner facing the wall, pretending she wasn't from Salt Lake at all, that she didn't have a son at East and one at Bryant, that her husband wasn't an accountant, that, somehow, there wasn't *something* bothering her heart at all.

It was when she arrived home that she saw Jim in the tub.

She had driven home in a rush of Iron Maiden songs and found another *New Era* in the mail, a magazine her mother subscribed to for her, and it had been the limit. She took it, gathered the three others that sat politely on the coffee table and threw them in the garbage beside the patio. Tyler, the family's sheepdog, came bounding from his nap; if Glenna was moving this fast, it must mean play. He jumped up on her. It was bad timing. She swiped him across the ears with her fist, almost screaming: "Get away from me!"

In her state, near tears, she cut through the boys' bathroom to reach her bedroom, and that's when she saw Jim, her fifteen-year-old, lying in the soapy water. He was reclining, his Walk-man earphones clamped on his head. The little machine sat beside the tub on a towel.

On seeing his mother march through, Jim started and said, "Mom?" way too loud in a tone that implied: *What's the matter?*

Even then it was too late. Glenna sat on her bed and thought: something's wrong. The image rushed her closed eyes: her son's long body floating, his white belly, his navel, the dark hair below in the soapy water. She couldn't figure it out, but she was mad, really mad. She was mad because her son had hair growing on his body.

She wanted to accuse Lance, her husband. "Did you know our son has pubic hair! Is this something you've arranged?" She sat on the edge of the bed and rocked back and forth slightly. She felt tragic and silly at the same time; she felt betrayed.

It didn't let up. Mark came home late from Bryant, and though Glenna had calmed herself, she still jumped him: "Where have you been? Feed your damn dog!"

"Mom," Mark said, sliding in to one of the kitchen chairs. "I've got to talk to you."

Mark was in a little trouble at school. He was halfway through his tale about the vice principal, when Jim came down the stairs dressed in his McDonald's uniform.

"Where are you going?" Glenna asked him.

"Mom," Jim said, opening his palms to model his outfit. "I'm going out to do drugs. What do you think? You know I work tonight. Carl's picking me up. He's out front right now. See you at eleven."

She turned back to Mark. He had "Oreoed" the vice principal's car, and he and three other boys had had to stay and wash the car, and they were going to be in detention the rest of the term, thirty minutes after school *every* day. Lance, her husband, walked in. He saw the looks on their faces and asked, "What's up?"

Glenna looked at Lance with the very look that said: "You're the author of all this misery." And she brushed by him on her way upstairs. What she did say was, "I'm sick of it. I'm sick of them. No more boys. No more dogs. You handle it."

That night, as a surprise to Lance, Glenna came on as a tigress. She covered his mouth every time he tried to speak, insisting that they just make love *her way*. At times it was strangely rough. Afterward, Lance rose on an elbow and asked, "Glen? Is there anything the matter? Glenna?"

Glenna knew something was happening. She found herself trying to remember the lyrics to Boston and Twisted Sister songs. She even knew she was self-conscious when she went to Nordstrom and bought whole outfits of Guess and Camp Beverly Hills. She wore her Guess sweatshirt around the house without a bra. Late one afternoon she stood at the sink singing, "I Want To Know What Love Is" along with Foreigner on the radio. She could see the stupid dog, Tyler, sitting in the backyard watching her, his head cocked to the side in what looked like sympathy.

In the evenings, she noticed that her sons avoided her when possible.



*LANCE* and Glenna went to cocktails at the Weymans'. The Weymans' children were grown, out of college, and lived in other cities. The Weymans were the oldest couple in the neighborhood. While Glenna looked forward to the party, she needled Lance about it, saying, "Oh yes, another gathering of the stodgy status quo."

"They're nice people, Glenna."

"They could get over that with the proper help."

It was a rather large gathering. The Weymans' house was filled. Glenna didn't know many people there, most were from the University. This was the party for Dr. Weyman's retirement. She left Lance with a group he played tennis with and scouted onward into the den, where she found her friend Mimi.

"Ah, basic black," Mimi said, nodding at Glenna's dress. "Your credo still is 'safety first,' right?"

Glenna liked Mimi, and seeing her, she was tempted to confess her pain, ask her, "Mimi, is there something happening to you?" But there was just enough jealously to prevent it. Mimi was four years younger, richer, and—Glenna thought—more clever. The two made fun of their husbands for a moment. Mimi had names for them: "Ordinary Lance" and "Dull Don," but when she looked through the archway, Lance was leading a small conversation and he looked handsome and animated. Don leaned against the mantel talking to two attractive women, members of the history department.

"Want to get stoned?" Mimi asked.

They went out the side door and sat in Mimi's Audi. It was cold in the car and the two passed the joint back for forth in silence. Glenna looked through the windshield at the ice hanging from the Weymans' garage. Finally, Mimi announced: "This is your life, Glenna!" Glenna looked at Mimi placidly and felt the panic of having another person read her mind. Then Glenna watched in alarm as Mimi said something Glenna knew she was going to say. Glenna felt she could see each word fall from Mimi's mouth, and Glenna felt how they lined up in the air and were at once right *and* obscene: "I saw Jim the other day," Mimi said. "He's quite a hunk."

Glenna snapped: "You stay away from my son!" And though she meant it and intended it as a grave warning, the two women began to laugh, to howl uncontrollably, laughing until there seemed no more air in the car. Glenna's stomach hurt from laughter and her jaw ached, when she turned in slow motion and saw the close-up of Lance's face outside her window. "Ahhhhhhhh!" Mimi screamed as she too saw the face, and the laughter tripled.

"Honey," Lance said to the closed window. "Honey, come in before you catch cold."

A moment later Lance was introducing Glenna to Jim's French teacher, Mr. Van Vliet. "I've always wanted to learn French myself," Glenna said, interrupting the compliment Mr. Van Vliet was making about their son. "Do you do any private tutoring?"

Sunday afternoon, Glenna sat alone on the kitchen table with her feet on a chair, nibbling Saltines, staring at Tyler out in the backyard. She had sent Lance, Jim, and Mark off to her mother's house.

"Why is Mom not going?" Jim had asked.

"Your mother has her reasons."

"And tell her to stop sending me magazines *and* do not bring back any clippings she's saved. I've had it with that stuff," Glenna had said.

"You've had it with a lot of stuff," Mark had said.

"That's enough, Mark."

"Well, Dad, it's true!"

"Let's just go. Let's just go to Grandma's," Jim had said.

"I'm bringing back the clippings," Mark had called from the front door. "I'm bringing them all!"

She had watched them climb into the car. Mark was still upset, Jim resigned, Lance dutiful. She had heard Jim say, as he pushed Mark into the backseat, "Forget it, big guy, she's having a little trouble with her *heritage*."

Glenna nibbled the crackers and rolled her eyes again, remembering his words. *Heritage*, for chrissakes. She stood, and Tyler in the backyard responded by standing too and waving his tail.

"No way," Glenna said to him, and moved to turn the radio on.

Mark arrived home from school just as Glenna was leaving for her first appointment with Mr. Van Vliet. Mark was doing better in school. The vice principal's car was okay; the Oreos hadn't damaged any of the paint. The vice principal had even admitted to the boys that in a way, a harmless prank could be funny. Mark stood on the front walk and watched the Volvo back down the driveway. Glenna saw him watching her. She rolled down her window. He just looked at her.

"Well?" she said finally. "What is it?"

"Mom," he said calmly, walking down to the car. "You're always running. I don't care that you don't talk to me. You're mad at me maybe. But Tyler's the family dog. You ought to be nicer to Tyler." In the cold air, his breath rose on both sides of his face. They looked at each other.

"I'll see you later," Glenna said to her son. "I'm late."

---

*MR. VAN VLIET* met Glenna at the door. "Can I get you something? Some coffee?"

"No coffee," she heard herself say. "But I'll take a drink."

As soon as he went into the kitchen and Glenna sat down, she felt like a fool. "French? I'm going to study French?" A flame of panic touched her throat.

Mr. Van Vliet returned with two coffee cups. "White wine. There's no other choice." Glenna tried to picture this man teaching her son's class, fussing over the roll, scolding a daydreamer.

The apartment was modern, primarily white. A framed poster centered each wall anouncing exhibitions of paintings in French. Stolen on summer sabbatical, she thought.

"Now," he sat down on a stool by the counter, "what makes you want to study French?"

Her throat constricted again, but she managed: "Oh . . . I've always wanted to. This seems like a good time for me." Then in her flooding nervousness a picture flashed in her mind. She was standing at cocktails with Mimi, saying, "Oh, yes, I'm taking French. It's *wonderful*." Glenna looked up at Mr. Van Vliet and said, "I'm not sure. If my son can learn it, can't I?"

"He's a good kid," Mr. Van Vliet said. "You did something right, something special to have such a good kid."

Glenna tried to sip the wine, but it tasted all wrong and she placed the cup on the end table.

Mr. Van Vliet smiled at her and said, "I'm sorry."

"No, it's fine wine, really. I'm just not sure if I have the discipline to study, to . . ."

"French can be a drag," he interrupted her. "Thank you for coming. I'm glad to see you, but you don't need French. You don't need a French tutor. You've got great kids."

Three days later, Glenna went to McDonalds. She parked next to the building where she could see Jim through the window. He was the tallest of the counter help. She saw him nodding amiably at the customers as he took their orders. She saw him flip the pencil and catch it and slip it behind his ear. Glenna sat in her car for twenty minutes watching the two little girls behind the counter with Jim smile and laugh and flirt with him. One took his nametag and pinned it on her shirt. Glenna put her hand to her face and felt herself smile. She turned off the radio and drove home.

LANCE planned a party. "It's what we need for these winter blues," he said to her.

"I haven't got the winter blues."

"Well, say I do. Come on. Let's have some people over."

MARK and Jim served the party. Lance and Glenna invited everybody they knew from work, the neighborhood, parents of their sons' friends.

"You boys look nice," Glenna said to her sons. They stood in the kitchen in their church pants and red vests. She reached and adjusted Jim's tie. "It's hard to get it straight because it's so narrow," she said.

"Want me to wear a tie, Mom?" Mark asked.

"No, I don't," she said, putting her hands on his shoulders. "I never want you to wear a tie." She looked closely at his face. "How old are you?"

"Eleven," he said.

"Going on five," Jim said, smiling.

"You boys know to serve . . ."

"From the left, Mom. Don't worry. Your family will not embarrass you."


AN hour later, the house was full. The Weymans. Robb Van Vliet came with Maria Del Prete, a Spanish teacher at East. Mimi arrived without Don.

"Mimi!" Glenna greeted her friend.

"Ah, the status quo in action. How's the party?"

"Fair. Nobody's stoned yet. Where's Don?"

"Dull Don will not be here."

Jim appeared at Mimi's left shoulder with a tray of shrimp. "From the left, properly, comes the shrimp. Madam, care for any?" he said.

"Hi, Jim," Mimi said. "None for me. I married one."

"Tut-tut," Jim said. "Your mouth! The way you talk." He moved away.

"He's so grown up," she said to Glenna.

Glenna looked at her friend, and without really thinking said, "We all are." The words seemed tangible in the air. Across the room she saw Mark hand Mrs. Weyman a glass of wine. For the first time she saw that he had the same fine shoulder-back posture as Lance, and then Lance was at her side, his arm around her.

"No drugs, ladies. There are children present." He kissed Glenna on the cheek.

Mimi made a little face. "I need a martini," she said moving away.

The party swelled into all the main floor rooms, shifted, and then sometime after midnight settled back into the living room where Lance was restoking the fire.

Robb Van Vliet and his companion, Maria Del Prete, had hooked up with Mrs. Weyman and Glenna, and they sipped brandy and laughed like old friends as Mrs. Weyman told stories about disastrous faculty parties at the University. Her tales wove back through the fifties and she told them each as little histories that held her listeners rapt. Glenna found herself again conscious of a kind of happiness, and she pressed her fingers to her lips as she smiled. It felt so good to laugh. When Mrs. Weyman finished the episode of "The Department Chairman and the Ice Bucket," Maria Del Prete said, "We don't have anything like that at our Christmas potlucks."

"This wicked woman is telling tales out of school," Mr. Weyman said. He had come up behind his wife's chair. "Don't deny it. I can tell by the scandalized look on everyone's face."

"I haven't started on you, dear. Don't worry."

Moments later, Robb Van Vliet rose and Maria Del Prete joined him. He told Glenna, "It's not too late to sign up for Spanish." He quickly held up his hand and said, "Just kidding. Thanks for the party. It was fun. You have nice friends."


*GLENNA* and Lance walked their last guests, the Weymans, home. "It's the first time we've been the last to leave a party in thirty years," Jack Weyman said.

"And it was a ball," Virginia said. The four of them stood in the street in front of the Weymans' in their coats talking for almost half an hour. Finally, Jack Weyman shook Lance's hand and Glenna gave Virginia a quick hug.

"We're going to San Diego Thursday," Jack Weyman said. "For a month. See if you can't get down for a long weekend. It's been a tough winter, and we'd love to have you."

Walking back, Glenna took Lance's arm. "That was fun. It *was* a ball. A good party."

"The Weymans are interesting people." Lance said.

"I want to see more of them."

"Really?"

"What do you mean, *really?*"

"They don't seem your . . ."

"They are!" Glenna said. "Call him tomorrow and tell him we'll come down in a week or two."

When they arrived home, Lance and Glenna found the boys doing dishes. "Wrong house," Lance said. "We've got the wrong house, Glen."

"Thanks, boys," she said. "Good work at the party. I don't know what I'd do without you." She walked to the patio door, still in her coat and went out into the backyard. Lance joined the boys in the dish assembly line. "She meant that, guys."

"Is she feeling better?" Mark asked.

"Check it out," Jim said, pointing a soapy cup out the kitchen window. There Glenna sat on the edge of the deck with her arm around Tyler. Tyler had his head on her shoulder. Her fur coat made it look like two dogs breathing into the icy night.

"It's a good sign," Mark said. "But I'm not convinced until she starts wearing her bra around the house. I'd like to bring some friends over again one of these years."

Portions of this book have appeared, sometimes in slightly different form, in the following: "The Governor's Ball" in *TriQuarterly*, a publication of Northwestern University; "The H Street Sledding Record" and "Blood" in *McCall's*; "The Time I Died" and "Max" in *Carolina Quarterly*; "Phenomena" in Writer's Forum; "Bigfoot Stole My Wife" in *Quarterly West*; "The Uses of Videotape" in *New Mexico Humanities Review*; "The Status Quo" and "Half Life" in *Network*; "Life Before Science" in *Fiction Network*.

Grateful acknowledgment is made to Folkways Music to reprint lyrics from © "The Lion Sleeps Tonight" (Mbube) (Wimoweh), new lyric and revised music by Hugo Peretti, Luigi Creatore, George Weiss and Albert Stanton. Based on a song by Solomon Linda and Paul Campbell. TRO Folkways Music Publishers, Inc. BMI.

## About the Author

Ron Carlson was born and raised in Utah. He taught and coached at The Hotchkiss School in Connecticut while writing his two previous books, *Betrayed by F. Scott Fitzgerald* and *Truants*. More recently, Mr. Carlson has made his home in Salt Lake City, serving as an artist-in-schools in Utah, Idaho, and Alaska. He is now writer-in-residence at Arizona State University and lives in Tempe with his wife and two sons and the good dog Max.